Gwendoline Keats

Life is Life

Other Tales and Episodes

Gwendoline Keats

Life is Life
Other Tales and Episodes

ISBN/EAN: 9783743364059

Manufactured in Europe, USA, Canada, Australia, Japa

Cover: Foto ©Andreas Hilbeck / pixelio.de

Manufactured and distributed by brebook publishing software (www.brebook.com)

Gwendoline Keats

Life is Life

LIFE IS LIFE

AND OTHER

TALES AND EPISODES

BY

ZACK

NEW YORK
CHARLES SCRIBNER'S SONS
1898

CONTENTS.

LIFE IS LIFE

PART I

CHIEFLY CONCERNING THE MAN ATTER

CHAPTER I

PAX INTRANTIBUS was carved on the great gates of Thursby Chase; but they sagged on their rusty hinges, and looked as if few cared to put their greeting to the test. The old Jacobean house, visible from a bend in the avenue, had an air of fallen fortunes; across the sleepy alleys grass crept undisturbed, and in the old-world gardens old-world flowers stretched up, cramped and cold, to the gaze of the October sun. Beech woods lined the back of the hill on which the house stood; below, in the valley, the river sidled, till the trees in their turn were displaced by gorse, then again by homely arable or quiet-faced pasture. Leaning against a stile, close to the river bank, was a thick-set, shrewd-faced man, dressed in corduroys and a brown velveteen jacket with deep, wide pockets. The sound of a sudden shot echoed across the river from the plantations opposite, and the man turned his head in that direction, and listened attentively.

"I didn't know that Sir John wor going to shoot they coverts to-day," he exclaimed.

A few minutes later a boy of about fourteen broke through the undergrowth, jumped the stile, and flung a pheasant at the man's feet.

"Wilkie," he said, "that sneak Bayles saw me shoot this."

"A phaysant, and a fine one," Wilkie remarked, turning the bird slowly over with his foot.

"What do you advise?" asked the boy, with a strong desire for maturer wisdom.

"Well, yer honour, if you vallers my advice," Wilkie answered, "you'll ate un fust and say he wor a rabbut arter."

"Oh!" exclaimed the boy, a little taken aback; "do you think that is a good plan?"

"The best I knows on, Master Humphrey," the man replied, "and now I reckon I'll be moving."

"Won't you stop and eat some of it your-self?" Humphrey asked, with a vague feel-ing that the impending feast might be pleas-anter if partaken of in company.

"I reckon not, yer honour, I reckon not," the man answered, moving away. "The bird once took, other folk's poaching is best left alone." He returned, however, after a few moments—"Ther's one thing," he said in a hoarse whisper, "burn the feathers for all you're worth." Having given this parting piece of advice he disappeared, seeming to melt into the trees.

"Look here," the boy called after him, "if you'll see me through, the next time I get half a sovereign I'll go shares with you." There was a faint rustle, and Wilkie thrust his face out through the undergrowth.

"Make it five-and-six and a pipe, yer honour," he said, "and I'll take the bird home and eat it myself."

"Will you?" replied the boy in a relieved voice. "It was a clean shot," he added, with a natural desire for commendation, as Wilkie dropped the pheasant into one of his capa-cious pockets.

" 'Twor so," the man answered. " You're the moral o' what yer father, the Cap'en, wor as a lad. He wud always a deal rather poach Sir John's coverts to shoot his own."

" You think I'm like him?" Humphrey replied, glowing. " Tell me about my father, Wilkie."

" You've heard the tale many a time, yer honour," the man answered with an indulgent smile.

" No matter," said Humphrey; " tell me everything, from the beginning straight on."

Wilkie took his pipe from his mouth, spat on the ground, and rubbed the spot clean with his boot. " Folks say," he began after a pause, " that the Thursbys an' Thursby have belonged to wan tother time out o' mind; but they've bin a free-handed lot, 'ave the Thursbys, an' wi' all rispact to yer, Master Humphrey, the place ain't what it wor; 'tain't possible, becase most of the money's gone, an' the land arter it; when the money goes the land vallers, an' thic mortal soon. Happen the Squire thought on that, baing alles turrible set on the Cap'en, yer father, marrying money; but, bless 'ee, he niver tooked to it, niver. There wor Miss Mary now, the darter of old Sir John, over to Trevorton, folks say as how she wor most powerful willin' towards yer honour's father; but he wudn't hear o' it, and wan night he an' the old Squire coomed to wuds; they wor turrible masterful, both o' 'em. Us niver knawed zackly what wor said, ony Mr. Henchel, ha that ba butler inter the house, tulled me a score o' times as how ha wor standin' in the hall when the Cap'en coomed droo.

" 'Pack my things, Henchel,' ha zed, 'I must git out of this.'

" Wull, wull, the Cap'en ha wint to Aus-tralie and died ther: a quare, lonesome place, as I've heard tell, wi' a deal o' nater about it. I windered to mesulf, as I drapped inter the charch this morning as they were a-openin' tha vault for his honour Squire Bellew's corpse, I windered to mesulf wuther the Cap'en wor slapin' sound over to furren parts, wi' maybe no stone a-tap o' him to keep him comfortable; but ther, ther, he wor alles wan o' yer ventursome wans; happen he wud as lief be up an' walkin' as bide quiet." Wilkie

was silent a moment. "Tha Almighty ba win-
derful fair-handed takin' Him all in all," he
continued meditatively. "Ther's the ginelfolks as has ther hatchments an' ther stones,
an' there's the pore man wi' nort maybe but
a daisy or so to mark un; but ha lies out
under the sky a deal nearer the Ressuraction :
ha won't 'ave no call to 'ammer this way an'
thic when the last trump sounds, for they
bury him mortal shaller nowadays, wi'out
much more than a sod twix ha and his Maker."

There was a long pause; the boy waited
with considerable patience; at last, however,
he interposed.

"But you haven't told all, Wilkie," he
said—" not the awfully interesting part."

"An' what part ba thic, Master Humphrey?"

"Oh, you know, where I come in, and
that ! "

A gleam of amusement flitted across the
man's face. "Shall I tull 'ee about the
poachin', or jest drap it ? " he asked.

Humphrey hastily considered the question.
"Tell all," he answered, "but cut the poaching rather short."

"Wull," Wilkie continued, "wan Christmas

night a matter o' dree years arter thic,—I minds the night wull becase that Mucksey laid hold o' me jest as I drapped upon a hare, an' I guv the piddlin' lump a bit of a scat an' brauk his arm."

"I think we'll skip the poaching," said the boy.

"As yer wull, Master Humphrey," Wilkie answered; "but the tale 'ull be all tags wi'out it. Happen the best knawed road's the shortest when coomes to heavy carting."

"Fire ahead," said the boy.

"I reckon 'twud ba as well to ern back to the beginning," Wilkie remarked, and recommenced accordingly. "Wan Christmas night——"

"Oh, bother the poaching! leave it out altogether," Humphrey interposed.

"Wiser not, Master Humphrey, wiser not."

The boy flung himself back impatiently on the coarse grass. "Tell what you like," he exclaimed, "only hurry up."

"Wull," Wilkie continued, "the Squire wor mortal put out about Mucksey's arm. They vussled me straight up to the house an' inter the buk-room. I wor always afeared o' buks, they ba such quietsome things; ther's no tulling what may be inside o' 'em.

" 'Well, Wilkie,' says the Squire, as soon as they great gapnesting[1] gawkins had been sent right about vace, 'what's this I hears about 'ee?'

" 'Happen, sir,' I answered, ' 'tis the breaking o' Mat Mucksey's arm yer mean; 'twor nort but a bit o' a westerpoop[2] I guved him. They Muckseys ba a vamily o' snippits ivery wan o' 'em.' I stapped an' fetched a bit o' breath, cuz 'twor mortal hard to find vitty wuds.

" 'Wull, Wilkie,' zed the Squire.

" 'Yer honour,' I tummled out, ' 'tworn't no drab o' a rabbit I wor arter that gaws dabbin' along wi' his nose to the ground.'

" 'Wull, Wilkie,' zed the Squire again. I ain't no friend to your varigated talkers, but dang me, Master Humphrey, if that there 'Well, Wilkie,' wasn't a deal more puzzlecacious.

" 'Yer honour,' I zed, 'ther's thic about a hare that draws a man on; happen 'twor a hare, happen 'tworn't.'

---

[1] Open-mouthed.　　　　[2] Knock.

"Then all to wance I seemed to find my tongue like.

"'Tain't the aitin' o' it, yer honour, but jest the doing o' it, that ba so powerful kindiddlin'.[1] When coomes to dealin' wi' natur a man needs ba mortal fingersome. Ther's yer snare now—none too high, none too low—an' the binding o' yer bit o' phaysant's grass. Belike 'tis a phaysant hisself yer arter, then yer must look to yer cord, cuz as sure as vath ha'll ern along the ground afore rising. Yer ginelfolks, yer pays yer pun's; yer buys yer phaysant eggs; yer lays down yer partridges, and yer rings 'em round wi' kapers, an' yer reckons yer have most graspit creation. But natur her slips droo yer fingers like water droo a sieve.'

"The Squire he turned away to the fire. 'Wilkie,' ha zed, sorter slow, 'if I let 'ee off this time, wull 'ee gie up poachin'?'

"It kind o' coomed to me tempting like to say 'Yes,' though I knawed sich promises cudn't be held; but ther ba a trustdrawsomeness about real ginelfolks that makes a man unusual truthful.

[1] Enticing.

" 'Yer honour,' I zed, 'poachin' is a kin-diddlin'[1] thing—a kindiddlin' thing.'

"Then he tarned an' looked inter my eyes, right down droo me, and I felt my heart give a great thud. 'Wilkie,' ha zed, 'ba 'ee afeared to be a man?'

" 'Yer honour,' I answered, ''ave 'ee iver swore to 'eezulf not to do a thing, an' kind o' zeed 'eezulf despisablelike an' low if 'ee shud do it, an' then gone strat an' dooed it jest the same? Ther's that in natur, yer honour, as won't be drove; an' I reckon the Almighty 'lows for thic when Ha coomes to make up a man's settling.' "

The old poacher paused and fell into a profound reverie; but the boy's face was full of suppressed excitement.

"Go on, Wilkie," he said; "you are coming to the best part of all."

"Wull," Wilkie continued, as he slowly loosened the tobacco in the bottom of his pipe with his knife, "I hadn't much more than laid out my tongue for the next wud when Henchel coomed in to say as how Dick Atter—he as wor the Cap'en's man—wanted

[1] Enticing.

to speak to the Squire most uncommon particular. I saw his honour turn a bit whitish.

"'Let him coome in,' he says, windervul
unconsarned, an' in Dick coomed accordin'.
His vace was mortal dyver'd,[1] an' looked
older by a good half-score years. He wor
karryin' a quare dumped up sorter skiddik;
but ha brought up his right hand to his face,
military fashion, turrible respactful.

"'What do 'ee want wi' me, my man?'
axed his honour.

"Dick he tooked a packet o' sommat from
his coat pocket; 'twor tied this way an' thic,
an' sealed most all over.

"'The Cap'en said I wor to give 'ee this,
sir,' he said.

"His honour cut the string, but his vingers
didn't zim none too clever at untying the
packet for all o' thic. Arter a bit, what shud
tummil out but the Cap'en's gold watch and
chain, an' a ring ha used to wear on the little
finger of his left hand!

"The Squire he guved a great start, an' his
face went reglar chalk-white. 'Where is
your master?' he axed, sharplike.

---

[1] Worn.

"'Dead, sir,' said Dick.

"His honour walked to. the winder an' stood an' stared droo the trees at the Black Swan lake that lay sorter gapnesting up at the sky. Arter a bit he tarned round.

"'Ther wor no message—nothing?' he axed.

"Dick put the big bundle down on a chair, an' arter a deal of unwinding o' stuff, what shud plump out but yer honour's self—a little snip o' a chile o' two year old, an' as sound aslape as a mole o' Christmas.

"'The Cap'en said I wor to tell 'ee, sir, that ha be a Thursby an' a ginelman,' said Dick, turrible respactful.

"I wor that tooked aback. 'Begore!' I rapped out, the wud slipping droo my teeth unconscious. His honour tarned round; I reckon ha had most forgot I wor ther. 'Wait in the servants' hall till I ring for 'ee,' said ha; an' I wor foced to go, tho' I wud 'ave gied a deal to 'ave bided."

"It was an awful pity you said 'Begore!' just then, Wilkie," the boy exclaimed.

"'Twor so, Master Humphrey."

There was a pause. "And my mother,

Wilkie," the boy asked, "you never heard anything about her?"

"Niver nort whatsoiver, yer honour."

"And Atter?"

"Ay, Dick?" the old poacher exclaimed in an aggrieved voice.

"What did he do?"

"*Do?*"

"Yes."

Wilkie withdrew his pipe from his mouth and spat on the ground. "Hiked[1] away an' niver zed a wud to wan o' us," he answered, returning the pipe to his mouth and chewing the stem with badly suppressed wrath. There was a pause, and the old poacher slowly puffed himself back into a calmer mood.

"'Tworn't much loss, ther wor more beer for better folk," he exclaimed, and relapsed again into silence.

The boy picked up a bit of moss, rubbing it to pieces between his fingers. "Why do you think Dick Atter went away like that?" he asked at length.

Wilkie brought his right hand down on his thigh with a resounding whack.

[1] Went.

"Many a time I've axed meself thic, Master Humphrey," he said. "Happen he wor afeared of that stratch-gallip tongue o' his."

Humphrey jumped to his feet with a quick impatient movement.

"I don't understand," he said.

The old poacher eyed him standing there, a well-built lad enough, broad at the shoulders, slim at the hips, the face keen, sensitive, with a promise of will in the cut of the chin. Wilkie seemed on the point of speaking, then changed his mind, once more withdrawing the pipe from his mouth, examined the old clay from bowl to stem before refixing it in a gap between two formidable, yellow, time-worn teeth.

"Dick Atter's a rapscallious lump; that ba my 'pinion," he remarked at last.

"You always say that, Wilkie," the boy answered with visible impatience, "but you never tell me *why* you think so."

"When a man's rapscallious, ha's rapscallious, Master Humphrey."

"What has he done?"

"Ther ain't no call to say what ha's dooed. I said ha wor a rapscallious lump; them wor my wuds, Master Humphrey."

"Yes," replied the boy, mounting colour, "and you're hitting a man that can't defend himself—hitting below the belt, too."

"Belike yis; belike no."

"Wilkie," exclaimed the boy, surprised out of his anger, "I don't believe you understand what I mean by hitting below the belt!"

"Belike yis; belike no," repeated the old poacher with a stolid indifference that Humphrey found extremely irritating.

"It's—it's dishonourable," he stuttered, and coloured at repeating the insult in cooler blood.

"Happen it ba; happen it baint."

Wilkie's indifference once more set the boy's rage floundering. "If a man called me dishonourable," he exclaimed, "I would knock him down like a shot."

The old poacher's eyes twinkled. "Law bless 'ee, Master Humphrey," he answered, "I let 'ee say yer say, yer ain't nought but a snip o' a chil'."

This new view of the situation somewhat disconcerted Humphrey, and he changed the subject.

"I hope some day to meet Atter myself,"

he said; "I've an awful lot to thank him for."

Wilkie searched in the tail-pocket of his old brown velveteen coat for an imaginary handkerchief; finding none, he blew his nose in a more primitive fashion. This, the sole comment on Humphrey's remark, the boy found out of all proportion irritating.

"Well, Wilkie," he said, in an annoyed voice.

"Nought, Master Humphrey."

"I think Atter is a brick myself," the annoyance visibly on the increase.

No answer. The old poacher lifting up his left foot, examined the sole of the boot with minute attention.

Humphrey's annoyance went full bound towards the brim. "There's nothing I wouldn't do for Atter if I had the luck to meet him," he exclaimed.

Again no answer. Wilkie transferring his scrutiny from the left to the right boot, the examination being if possible more minute.

"I will just tell you what," said the boy in a fierce voice, "the very instant I'm of age, —the very instant, mind,—I will go straight

away, find Atter, and *thank* him. I should like
to hear what you've got to say to that, Wilkie?"

"Nought, Master Humphrey; nought
whatsoiver."

Unconsciously the boy clenched his fists.
" I should just advise you to say something,"
he exclaimed, a sudden huskiness coming into
his voice.

Grim amusement was visible on the old
poacher's brown, leathery, deeply-wrinkled
face as he slowly looked the boy all over.
" Ay," he answered, " but women, childer,
an' vools ba maist wan."

"I think we had better part, Wilkie, before I am tempted to do you an injury,"
said the boy, trembling with rage.

" Wull," exclaimed the old poacher, rising
and stretching himself, " I reckon I shud ba
getting along; Farmer Rod, over to Chope,
axed me to be down wi' tha tarriers a matter
avor dree: tha ba gwaying to drash them
corn-ricks: ther 'ull ba a sight o' rats, I
reckon—a sight o' rats."

Humphrey, who had moved away, slack-
ened pace: the old poacher glanced at him
out of the tail of one eye.

"Us killed 'em by the score last year," he said; "vleas cudn't wull 'ave been thicker."

Humphrey pulled up dead short; back, however, still turned in Wilkie's direction.

"Ay," remarked the latter, "'twor purty sport: a man had to keep his eyes unbuttoned an' lay about him mortal smart or wan o' they rats wud ba up tha leg o' his trousers in less time than Varmer Rod's old white drake takes to shake his tail."

Humphrey wheeled straight round. "I was thinking," he said, "of going to Chope myself."

"Then us had better ba gittin' along, yer honour."

As they moved away the boy's thoughts still jingled with Dick Atter's story.

"Wilkie," he said, "what do you think my mother was like?"

"I niver zeed hur mysulf, Master Humphrey, an' niver drapped across no pusson that had, for the matter o' that," the old poacher answered. "Happen hur wor powerful white about the vace an' hands; leastways that ba how I've alles reckoned hur,— ginelfolks baing sich."

"Who told you that my mother was dead?" demanded the boy.

"No wan whatsoiver, Master Humphrey."

"Then——"

The old poacher glanced at him with a good deal of kindly pity.

"I reckon hur's dead, pore soul," he said at last. "I wudn't ba arter worrying hur if I wor 'ee, Master Humphrey; happen her wud liefer bide quiet."

There was a long pause, and when the boy spoke again his voice had a certain huskiness.

"I think, Wilkie," he said, "that ratting, after all, is tame sport. I'll go back to the house and splice my rod." He turned away, suddenly to wheel round towards the poacher, his face flushing.

"I was rather angry just now, wasn't I, Wilkie?" he asked, giving a fierce twiddle to one of his jacket-buttons.

"Nought worth mentioning, yer honour."

Humphrey gave a gulp. "Well, I regret it," he said; "but," brightening, "you can't box, can you, Wilkie?"

"No, yer honour."

"Well, I expect I should have made things unpleasant for you."

"May be, yer honour, may be," the old poacher answered; "and as for Dick Atter," he continued, "ha ba a rapscallious lump for sure"—Humphrey winced,—"but happen ha acted fair by yer honour, an' us 'ull let the rapscalliousness bide over accordin'."

The tears shot into the boy's eyes. He held out his hand; what he said, however, might to an ordinary mortal have sounded somewhat inconsequent.

"I am coming on Sunday," he remarked in a casual tone, "to look at the ferrets; afternoon church time. Don't forget, Wilkie."

"Right yer are, Master Humphrey," the poacher answered; "an' ther's a bit of fair-in', my old dummon bought inter Moulton, awaitin' for 'ee a-tap the dresser."

The two separated, and Wilkie, turning back, glanced for a moment at the boy's retreating figure. "Ay, but Dick Atter," he muttered. "Wull, wull, he had his good points the same as the rest; when it coomed to paying the score, your glass was as good as his own."

CHAPTER II

It was a mild spring evening some four years later. The park and lawns, dew-thick in moonlight, lay glistening like the blade of a fresh-sharpened scythe, and upon them gigantic shadows spread out long arms. A faint scent of the night primrose drifted against the Chase windows; but the shutters were closed, and the scent could not enter. Humphrey was seated opposite the Squire, over his wine; the further end of the great dining-hall was lost in shadow, against which the lights from the candelabra beat vainly. High up over his head the carved ceiling looked as grim and as far away as the age in which it had been designed. On the walls hung the portraits of Thursbys, dead, —all but the eyes, which, ever alert, peered down upon the boy. Humphrey glanced at the Squire sipping his wine, and wondered what were his thoughts: was he, too, haunted by those ever-vigilant eyes, or had he grown indifferent with years?

After a while the Squire pushed back his chair. "Well," he exclaimed, rising from the table, "it will be some time before we dine again together, I suppose. I'm sorry; but if you will colonise—you will."

"I am sorry to leave you too, sir," Humphrey answered, following his grandfather into the smoking-room; "but I have made up my mind to find that fellow Atter and sift his story to the bottom."

"You are not likely to succeed where the detectives failed," replied the Squire. Lighting a cigar, he puffed at it a few moments in silence. "Best leave the past alone, my lad," he added.

Humphrey turned on him with quickened pulses. "I know very little of that past, sir," he said.

"You share in the general ignorance."

"But I know *nothing*."

There was a moment's pause. "And I also," said the Squire.

"What!" exclaimed Humphrey, startled out of himself, "you know *absolutely nothing?*"

The Squire turned away. "Isn't it rather late to discuss such a subject?" he said.

"The truth means a great deal to me, sir," Humphrey answered.

" Ah—the truth ! "

" Yes."

The Squire laid a hand on Humphrey's shoulder. " My lad," he said, "Atter's story was as impossible to prove as disprove."

Humphrey's face went chalk-white. " But, but, but," he stuttered and stopped short,— the words stuck in his throat; pride prevented him asking if the Squire believed him his grandson. Standing there, however, the question ran like a red-hot wire through his brain.

" You acknowledged me on slender evidence," he said at last.

"And have not regretted it so far," the Squire answered. " I admit," he continued after a pause, " that I might have done otherwise, had I known from the first how difficult Atter's story might prove to authenticate."

Humphrey shuddered, and hated himself for shuddering. " I feel a Thursby, sir," he said, " every bit of me."

The Squire smiled. " Yes, yes," he answered; " I think we all know that."

"You are certain Atter went back to Aus-tralia?" Humphrey asked, suddenly.

"Yes. We traced him to New South Wales; but there is very little chance of your coming across him."

"I have a premonition that I shall run up against him. You don't believe in premonitions, I expect, sir?"

"No, not much."

"He was a well-built man, you say?"

"Yes; a great muscular fellow, with rather a fine face, and had, I should imagine, a devilish temper of his own."

"And as to trustworthiness?"

"Personally, I knew very little of the man; but your father thought well of him."

"Did he impress you that night as a man who was speaking the truth?"

"Yes," said the Squire, moving away, "he told his story in a straightforward manner; but it is possible that I was not at that moment the best of critics."

The Squire's voice trembled, and he went to the window and, flinging back the shutters, stared across the park, where the moonlight slept and the Black Swan lake held up a shadow-soaked face to the sky.

"It must all come to the hammer," he exclaimed half aloud.

Humphrey caught the words. "Not inevitably," he answered, almost unconscious that he had spoken.

The Squire glanced at him. "It is mortgaged up to the hilt," he said. "At least, most of it."

"But I may fall on my feet in Australia," Humphrey answered, blushing boyishly.

The Squire smiled. "By the way," he said, "I think I told you that I had a very fair offer for the Chope and Marston farms, which I have decided to close with. Well, I propose, after the mortgages have been paid off, placing the balance in some sound investment; the whole sum, including interest, to be paid over to you when you reach the age of twenty-five. It will be no great sum— some few thousands, probably; but by that time you will have been able to look round and have gained sufficient experience to make the most of it."

He was silent a moment. A hundred

different ideas buzzed off like fireworks in the boy's brain. It seemed to Humphrey as if this promised money was all that was needed to found the fortune with which the Chase was to be saved.

"There is only one objection," he said, in a voice trembling with excitement.

"And that is?"

"Something might turn up before I was twenty-five. You see, sir," he continued excitedly, "the colonies are not like England; a man has twice the chance there that he has here. I heard a fellow saying the other day that, with a little money and a decent head-piece, success was a practical certainty."

"H'm," said the Squire.

"You'll allow I'm no fool," said Humphrey, with the proud conviction that he was a very clever fellow indeed.

"It depends very much on the kind of fool you mean," was the Squire's unexpected reply.

"Oh—ah!" exclaimed Humphrey, much taken aback; "I don't think fool is quite the right word, sir. One might put it that I have as much brains, perhaps more, than the general run of fellows."

"Well," replied the Squire, smiling, "suppose we put it that way; what follows?"

"Then," said Humphrey, with an unconscious ring of triumph in his voice, "the chances are that I shall make a big pile. If only——" he stopped short.

"Well?"

"I'm given a free hand, sir."

"What do you understand by a free hand?"

"Do you really intend the money you spoke of for me?"

"Certainly."

"Well, give it to me outright; not when I am twenty-five, but now."

"You would lose every penny of it before you had been in Australia six months."

"I'm not an *absolute* fool, sir."

"My dear lad," replied the Squire, laughing, "perhaps if you thought yourself one, there would be more hope for you."

A dead pause. Humphrey kicked the rug with his foot.

"Well," exclaimed the Squire at last, "tell me your plans."

Humphrey brightened, he walked across to

the window where the Squire stood. " I talk
as if I were awfully cock-sure of myself; but
you understand, don't you?" he said apolo-
getically. Their eyes met, and the Squire
placed his arm in the boy's.

" Now tell me the plans," he repeated.

Humphrey glowed. " Well, what I should
suggest," he exclaimed, in an important voice,
" is that the money should be placed at de-
posit in some good colonial bank, say the
Bank of Australasia (they gave you four
per cent some time back—they don't now,
though); and then, if any really good thing
turned up, I should be in a position to take
advantage of it. You see, sir, having the
money on the spot might make all the difference between a big or a small success. I
heard that fellow I was telling you about say
that he had the chance once of an absolutely
sure thing, thousands in it, and he kept telegraphing and telegraphing home to his people (he was hard up, too, and had to pay ten
shillings a word); just as he reached his last
sovereign, back came the answer, and, would
you believe it, sir, all it said was—' Go to the
devil.' "

The Squire chuckled.

"That is not giving a fellow a chance, is it?"

"Not the ghost of one," replied the Squire, still chuckling.

"I am glad you see it in the right light, sir."

"Yes," admitted the Squire humbly, "I think I do."

"I can have the money, then?" very eagerly.

"Well, well," answered the Squire, "I must think about it: I should be doing you a very bad turn, I am afraid, by consenting."

There was a long silence. "I have never told you," said Humphrey at last with a kind of gulp, "but, but I think rather a lot of the Chase myself; and, and one of the principal reasons why I want the money is, is—I'm rather a fool at explaining; but, but——" he stopped dead, his eyes swimming.

"I understand," said the Squire shakily, "I understand." His grasp on the boy's arm tightened, and they both stood silent, looking out over the lands so dear to the heart of each of them. At this moment the butler entered.

"If you please, sir," he said, addressing Humphrey, "Wilkie is here and is anxious to see you."

"Tell him to come in, Henchel," Humphrey answered, and after a brief interval the old poacher entered.

He was carrying a long, curiously-shaped parcel. "A present to you from the parish, yer honour," he said, placing the parcel on the ground, where it stood up stiff and straight.

"What is it?" asked Humphrey with some curiosity.

"No hurry, yer honour, no hurry; I ain't unpacked 'em yet," replied the poacher, unwinding the paper covering.

"Good heavens!" ejaculated the Squire, "a pair of trousers. What are they made of? Why, they stand upright of themselves!"

"The best leather in the parish, yer honour," answered Wilkie, whisking away the last bit of paper from one of the legs. "The village thought they would be mortal handy over to furren parts, where sich things be scarce, so to speak. There's a deal o' wear in 'em," he continued, turning the trousers round, with the air of a connoisseur; "the

Jidgement Day 'ull find 'em much the same
as they be now."

The Squire chuckled. "So I should be
inclined to think," he said.

"Ay, ay, yer honour, there ain't been the
like o' sich a pair o' trousers in the parish
afore," the poacher continued, glowing with
a showman's justifiable pride; "but the village is more eddycated than it wor since they
penny readings and village councils coomed in.
Five years agone Thursby wudn't have knowed
that Australie wor such a terrible place for
thorns. At least so folks wor saying down
at the Thursby Arms. Parson Jack's man
stid the trousers up on the counter, and the
whole parish coomed in jest to look at 'em."

"It is awfully good of you all," said Humphrey, with a suppressed groan. "Do you
think you could carry them up-stairs for me,
out—ah—out of this?"

"Law bless yer honour," Wilkie answered, "that tiddlewinkie spit o' doo that
be coming droo the winder won't wark 'em
no harm."

Again the Squire chuckled audibly.

"No, no," Humphrey answered, reddening,

3

" but they will have to be packed. Wait in my room till I come up," he added, dropping a sovereign into the old poacher's hand.

Wilkie pulled his forelock. " I wud have taken good care o' em wi'out that," he answered; " but there," he continued, looking down on the gold piece, " health is better than wealth, and a sovrun's a sovrun; I humbly hopes I sees you hearty, yer honour," so saying he raised the leather trousers once more to his shoulder and left the room.

The Squire watched him, smiling. " So I am to send all letters care of the bank at Sydney?" he asked, changing the subject.

" Yes; that would be the safest. You see it will be close on shearing-time when I reach the colonies, and I thought of trying to get work on some of the New South Wales sheep-stations; going from shed to shed as a rouse-about[1] would give me my best chance of coming across Atter."

" Well, my boy," said the Squire, flicking the ash off his cigar, " I can't help thinking

[1] Unskilled labourer; used sometimes as a term of contempt.

you would be wiser to let the affair drop altogether."

"I can't, sir—I would if it weren't for my mother; but, but—you see she might be— alive." The boy's eyes filled with quick tears, and he turned away to hide his emotion.

"As you will," said the Squire hurriedly— "as you will."

"I must, sir."

"Well, that settles it."

.   .   .   .   .   .

The following day Humphrey left England for Australia.

PART II

THE MAN ATTER

CHAPTER I

IT was summer on one of the New South Wales border stations. The roof of the big corrugated iron wool-shed lay like molten lead beneath the sun, and the heat reeled off it and fought the ammonia stench and red dust-clouds rising from the sheep-yards. Inside the thermometer fizzled at a few degrees lower; there was no dust; the floor, white and polished as a bread platter, was littered with soft yolky fleeces. To all appearance the shed was empty: shearer and rouse-abouts, having struck work and declared for the Union, were filing, swag on shoulder, quart-pot and water-bag in hand, across the plain towards their new camping-ground some distance down the creek. Moving by, the

sound of their voices clattered against the
shed walls; and a boy, who lay concealed behind a heap of fleeces, raised himself cautious-
ly and glanced out at them. He was a straight-
limbed young fellow verging on manhood, and
looked, in spite of his ragged jumper and
tarred moleskins, a gentleman. As Humphrey, for it was he, stood watching, four
men broke off from the rest, and, after a short
consultation, came towards the wool-shed.
The boy's heart thumped against his ribs, but
he made no further attempt at concealment;—
the strikers walked up the gangway, pushed
back the door and entered. They were strong-
built men, lean, wiry, well-seasoned — each
more than a match for the boy; they knew
their superiority and made him feel it, as they
bound his hands and sent him out of the shed
with a rousing kick. He glanced across the
great red dusty plain with its trail of red-
eyed dusty shearers; there was no living soul
among them who would stand his friend; he
straightened his shoulders and determined to
stand by himself. Leaving the main track
the men forced him to enter the scrub, where
the tall, rank crab-grass marked the course of

the last flood and hid the cracks and holes in
the ground. The boy stumbled awkwardly,
and the men laughed and kicked him so that
he stumbled again; then he set his teeth and
planted his feet with care, for too much kicking is bad for the blood. Reaching the camp,
his appearance was greeted with jeers of
derision.　　　　　　　　　.

"Here's your ha'porth of milk, Bullocky,"
cried one of the men. The strike leader paid
no attention to the remark, but, striding up
to Humphrey, gripped his shoulder with the
force of a steel vice. Standing facing each
other, it was apparent that they were both
something of the same build; but the man's
figure was the finer, the firmer set, his chest
deeper and of greater girth, and he carried
his immense height with ease. The head,
well poised and finely moulded, was covered
with a thick crop of white hair; one deep
wrinkle cleft the forehead between the eyes;
the chin in its obstinate strength might have
been some devil's chin, but the mouth be-
trayed the weakness of a man rocked by
passions. For a moment neither spoke, the
gaze of their grey eyes tense as a tightly

strung steel wire. Then Bullocky relaxed
his grip. "Wot do yer mean by skulking,
yer blanked blackleg?" he exclaimed.

Again there was a silence; and the boy
picked mechanically at a piece of wool on his
blue jumper. He did not look a heroic figure
standing there with the mark of a recent kick
on the back of his moleskins, neither did he
feel heroic,—he felt something much nearer
akin to fear; but his quiet bearing distin-
guished him as belonging to a different class
from his tormentors.

"I do not believe in strikes," he answered
deliberately.

A ripple of surprise passed through the
men; they turned by instinct and glanced at
their leader's face—at his great jaw and
square-cut chin where the passion was frozen
solid, at the twitching mouth, at the over-
bearing, passion-ripped brow.

"Inter the creek with him, Bullocky; set
his blamed gullet a-wash," cried one of the
strikers.

Involuntarily the boy's glance strayed to
the creek. It lay some ten feet below the
bank,—a pleasant place enough to camp by

at noon or sundown, with the bell of your
hobbled horse clinking in your ear, and the
red-back shuffling lazily from under the lignum on to the black-faced water; pleasant to
lie and watch the ibis fishing solemnly, lifting one lean-shanked leg from the centre of
a round-rimmed ripple, to place it bang in
the centre of another; while far out on the
mirage-hunted plain the native companions
dance fantastic dances, the great bush-bustard
sails on awkward, rustling wings, and the emu
trots his wide-paced slinging trot with bob-
bing rump;—pleasant enough, but somehow
it did not look so to Humphrey as he scanned
its black, snag-broken surface.

Bullocky, seeing the direction of the glance,
laughed, and the men surged in closer. One
of them tied a rope round the boy's waist,
not to prevent drowning, but to prevent escape; a hundred hands tore at him, buffeted,
raised, shot him up and forth on what seemed
an everlasting journey through space; then
the angle of his flight changed, and he began
to fall downwards; again he seemed to feel
the hands, tearing at his vitals this time, till
with a crash he struck the water, which

closed over, crushing him in a heavy embrace. He was hauled ashore and lay with the wind knocked out of him, afraid, sickeningly afraid, not of the men, but of that long, long flight through the air, and those terrible, invisible hands that tore at his vitals as he fell down towards the sharp-edged water.

Bullocky came forward and stooped down, till the boy felt the man's hot, fetid breath upon his face.

"Well, you long-tongued, corn-stalking son of a kangaroo," he said, "have you had enough of preaching, or do yer want another dose of the creek?"

Tearing and plunging in Humphrey's chest a great sob rose, he fighting it back to silence, as he would have fought a devil; for Bullocky was watching, tracking the sob with triumphant scorn, and, when it broke bonds, stuttering out, kicked him very, very softly, in the way he would, when not drunk, have toed out his contempt on a woman.

The boy staggered to his feet. "You cowardly cur," he cried, "I will never give in to you."

A moment later and a blow, planted above the heart, sent him reeling into the creek; a snag struck his eyes, tearing away the sight. Two men went down the bank and brought him ashore, and he lay limp as a corpse before it is death-stiffened.

"He looks sorter dead," exclaimed one of them, drawing back. "You hit him over the heart, Bullocky."

The strike leader turned his fear-sodden face on the speaker. "Git out o' this," he cried, "or, by the living God, I'll lay yer out the same!"—and the man slunk away through the trees. The blood began to ooze from under the boy's closed eyelids, and one of the strikers brought some water in his hat, and stood looking at Bullocky, the water dribbling from the hat on to the boy's blue jumper. Bullocky Dick knelt down, opened the jumper and placed his great, coarse, trembling hand over his victim's heart. After a while he beckoned to the man.

"See if he's pegged out; my hand's kind o' shaky," he said: his voice had a stiff sound as if it worked on unoiled hinges.

The man ripped the jumper and shirt wider

back, and laid his ear down against the lad's
heart; shearers and rouse-abouts came a step
forward, gripping at their breath; Bullocky
stared across the creek at the lignum scrub.

There was a moment's silence, then the man
turned a twitching face to the strikers.

"The blood in my head is so blanked noisy,
I can't tull," he said.

Another man came forward, knelt down,
raised the boy's eyelids, dropped them, and
exclaimed, "Not dead;—blinded!"

A ripple of relief ran through the strikers;
then they glanced at the bleeding eyes, shuddered, slunk back, humped swags, and moved
off through the trees, leaving their leader and
his victim alone. Bullocky Dick stood, his
face swept clean of passion; turning, he saw
his late followers in full retreat, and burst
into a laugh that sent the men, shuddering,
faster on their way. His horse was hitched
by the bridle to a tree close by; mounting,
he rode off in the direction of the nearest
Bush public.

The moon was up when he returned; the
dry sapless grass lay white beneath it, and
the ring-barked gums, lining the creek's edge,

stood whiter. The boy had regained consciousness, and half rolled, half slipped down
the bank, knelt bathing his eyes.

Silently Bullocky watched him try to climb
up the bank, miss his way among the roots,
and slide back once more towards the creek.
Dismounting, Bullocky carried his victim to
the foot of a great half-dead gum-tree, and
propped him with his swag against the trunk.

The boy murmured thanks. " Who are
you ? " he asked, turning his sightless, blood-
stained face towards the strike leader. There
was a long silence; a brown wood-duck shot
down upon the creek, and, skating forward
on her breast, threw up a great triangular
ripple behind on the level black water.

" In the old country they called me Dick
Atter," said Bullocky at last.

A spasm of pleasure crossed the boy's face;
he raised himself.

" A man called Dick Atter once did me a
great service," he exclaimed eagerly. " I've
always wanted to meet and thank him. I
suppose you can't be he? My name is
Thursby, one of the Thursbys of Thursby,
Devonshire. Do you know the name ? "

"Yes," replied Atter, "I know the name."

"Well, I'm Humphrey Thursby, Captain Thursby's son. 'Twas you who brought me home from Australia. I must have been a fine nuisance; but it's pleasant meeting you at last."

Atter made no reply. Sitting there, he seemed to age between one splash of moonlight and the next; in twenty seconds he grew older by as many years; his lips formed words, muttering, muttering, but no sound broke the silence.

"Those brutes have knocked me about rather badly," the boy continued; "I must get down to Bourke,—the doctor will soon patch me up; I'm blind now, but it can't be permanent. A fellow's career isn't destroyed quite so easily—eh, Atter?"

Still no reply. Humphrey dragged himself forward and laid his hands on Atter's knees. "You *are* the man I mean?" he asked. "You served under my father in the 4th, eh?"

No answer.

"You don't seem quite to understand; I'm——"

Atter burst into a loud, terrible laugh.

"Yer ain't no bloody Thursby," he exclaimed;
"you're my son, and I've blinded yer."

"You lie in your throat!" cried Humphrey, and fainted, his head striking Atter
across the chest as he fell forward.

The moon rose higher and the earth grew
whiter in her embrace. A flock of gulars,
startled by Atter's laugh, had flown chattering out from a ring-barked gum, and chattering back, they stuttered a moment, and
then fell to silence and to sleep, leaving the
dying tree to stare down its dishevelled sides
at the bark-littered ground. Atter pushed
the boy from him and searched the roll of
swag till his trembling hand found, and drew
forth, a bottle of spirits—Bush whisky. He
drank and drank, but did not become drunk;
he became vividly, keenly, awfully awake:
but Humphrey lay unconscious, unheeding,
and around him the Bush, with its sapless
grass and shadeless trees, trembled in the
cooler air of dawn.

CHAPTER II

It was noon two days later; some hundred strikers were collected near an entrance-gate of the station: stretching out, a long line in front of them, the main track between Bourke and Brewarrina wound now across a hard red plain, now sunk in mealy soil, grey-brown and studded with holes like a pepper-pot lid. There was no wind, the narrow leaves of the mulga hung down stiff and awkward; across the plain, under mounted police convoy, three coaches rolled steadily forward; on top of them and inside, thick as flies, swarmed the " free labourers." The coaches drew nearer, and a hail of sticks (the plain did not boast of stones) fell on them; the police drew their revolvers, they had orders not to fire, and the coaches continued to advance. Towards them rode Atter, behind him heaved the strikers, cursing as only an Australian can curse, till the air seemed rank beneath its load of impious filth.   Whirling a great stock-whip round his head, Atter struck a trooper's mare across the eyes: the maddened animal dashed into a wire fence, tore free, flinging her rider. Cut to the bone, and with half a yard of wire banging at her legs, the mare went careering towards the creek,—a moment later she had jumped the bank, a submerged snag caught the bridle, dragging her down; for a while the poor brute spun round, then sank screaming beneath the water. Meanwhile the strikers had rushed the coaches,—seething up over the sides, a kicking, biting, limb-tearing swarm,—till the great coaches rocked, and every man upon them had become a solid Unionist before the drowning mare had ceased to scream. Then the strikers and their new allies went amicably away in the direction of the nearest Bush public, there to drink to- gether to the general and particular discom- fiture of the " blanky squatter." The police trooper who had been thrown from his horse struggled to his feet; he had been knocked a bit silly, and began laughing in a mad, aim- less fashion, going up and down like a bell- rope. Atter watched the man a moment, then sent a piece of mulga whizzing towards him; it struck the side of his head, and he fell with

the laugh choked out of him. The strikers
grinned appreciation, but Bullocky, with his
face set like a stone, left his companions and
rode away in the direction of his own camp.
Outside the tent, his head supported on his
arm, Humphrey lay asleep: the flies swarmed
across and around his bandaged face. Atter
looked at him awhile, sat down, filled his pipe,
and began smoking. The flies buzzed; Humphrey rolled to one side, sighing heavily.
Atter glanced at him again: the boy, with his
mouth relaxed by sleep, looked very boyish,
and the man's hard brutal face became less
hard, less brutal. He picked up a bunch of
twigs, switched the flies away; they swarmed
back, and he sat smoking and switching, and
the boy fell into a sounder sleep. At last
Humphrey awoke. Putting up his hand instinctively to his eyes, he tried to rearrange
the bandage; Atter leaned over to where his
roll of swag lay, untied the bundle, fished
out a clean shirt, and tearing off a strip from
the tail, flung the piece of linen towards the
boy.

"There," he said, " tie 'em up wi' that."
He watched the boy's vain, awkward efforts

4

to find the linen; then, leaning forward, folded and tied the fresh bandage for him, his great coarse fingers shaking rather oddly.

"Blank me," he exclaimed, with a half laugh, "tarring stud ewes[1] after shearing is nothing to yer."

Humphrey turned his bandaged face towards the sun.

"I must get down to Bourke," he said wistfully.

"To the hospital?"

"Yes."

"Ah—well," exclaimed Atter, "I reckon that this bally place will soon be a blanked sight too hot to hold me."

Humphrey had an intense longing to escape from the man,—to get away somewhere and think.

"I could coach down," he said, "if you would see me as far as Ryan's,"—Ryan's was the name of the nearest Bush public.

The strike leader picked up a stick and sent it after a great pink and grey iguana that was scuttling up a gum-tree.

---

[1] Tarring stud ewes, &c. The wounds of a sheep caused by the slipping of the shears are always tarred.

"No," he answered, after a pause, "I reckon I'll run yer straight into the yards myself."

There was a long silence. Humphrey shifted his weight from one elbow to the other.

"Atter," he exclaimed at last, "you owe me an explanation."

"Then yer blanked well won't git it."

"Yes," cried the boy fiercely, throwing himself upon the man, "by God, you shall answer me."

Atter shook him off as he would a fly. "None o' that," he answered. Then, after a pause, "Wot do yer want to know?"

"The truth at last—whether I am a Thursby or——"

"Go an' be a blanked Thursby if yer like; I'll never blab on yer: her reckoned 'ee one, any way."

"Who do you mean by 'her'?" asked Humphrey, his voice trembling.

"Ther wuman."

"What woman?"

Atter cursed. "Your mother," he answered sullenly.

Humphrey's head sank down upon his

hands; he remembered over again how often
he had drawn mental visions of his mother,
from whom he had so long been parted, and
now he lay beside the black-faced creek and
wondered, trembling.

"Atter," he said at last, lifting up his face,
"I came to Australia to find her—to claim
her."

"She's dead."

"Dead?"

"Yes."

The boy gave a short cry. "Where?
How did she die?"

"Died mad."

"Mad!"

"Yes."

"My God! Atter, tell me the truth; you
owe it to me."

Bullocky was silent; the wrinkle that
clove his brow sank deeper, and on his hard
brutal face mental suffering scrawled deep
lines.

"Gawd help me! I can't tell yer," he exclaimed at last.

The boy sank his head down once more
upon his hands, and there was silence. Sud-

denly Atter began to speak in a thick, stuttering voice—not to the boy, but as if to some invisible auditor.

"Wot's a wuman?" he said. "Wot's a blank wuman? Wot's one wuman more than another?"

He stopped short, and sat staring straight in front of him; a pair of bronze-winged pigeons fluttered down, pecking at the dried grass-roots near the camp.

"Hur wos poor," he began again, "poor as any cockatoo's wife,—an' wot's a blanked wuman when hur's poor?"

Again he fell silent; the bronze-winged pigeons flew away.

"If her ain't a bad un, her should be," he exclaimed bitterly; "if her ain't a bad un, her should be. 'Tis her own fault if her ain't; her wudn't suffer then. Wot's a wuman, any way?

"'Twas on board ship I saw her first, on the voyage out. Her was a second-classer, same as myself. I was servant to Cap'en Thursby in they days. Her wasn't nort speshil about the face,—I've seen scores o' women as 'ad beat her for looks; but her wos

sorter different from other women, sorter different, sorter different," he repeated to himself, "sorter different. I took to watching her
kind o' casual. I got a feeling somehow as if
her shouldn't have bin there—as if her shud
o' bin on the main deck olong o' the leddies.
Then I wud look at her dress—'twas a pore,
thready, rain-crinkled affair—and say to myself, 'Can't be'; an' the next minet, maybe,
her wud git up an' walk across the ship, an'
I'd know by the way of her moving that her
was one o' em——" He stopped short, adding
abruptly, "They be all women, same as the
rest. An' wot's a wuman? Wot's a wuman
when hur's poor? Wot's a wuman, any
way?" and fell back again to staring across
the black-faced creek.

"Ay, blank 'em!" he exclaimed, "I niver
thort much o' wimen meself. Whistle and
they'll come to 'ee, most o' 'em; an' the more
you kick 'em, the more they'll lick yer hands.
But her—— Arter a bit, I took to wishing
her was the same as the rest; I wanted her
badly, an' ther was a blanked line atween us
that I couldn't cross, do wot I wud. I said
to myself, 'Wot's this blamed line you have

got hold of in yer head, Dick Atter ? Ther
ain't none such ; the wuman's dirt poor. A
man who was a man wud take her, use her,
and fling her away.' But the line was atween
us, the line was atween us.

"One day 'twas cold and rough, and the
blanked ship rolling fair to split her sides;
most o' the passengers was sitting wi' chairs
lashed up agin the hatchways, and all their
spare swag planked on top o' 'em; but her
stud, kind o' hunting for shelter. Ivery now
and then the wind 'ud come full on her, reg'lar
licking her thin clothes up agin her legs : her
hadn't got no speshil chair the same as the
rest. All to once the Cap'en—Cap'en Thursby
—came along. He was a wild un, was the
Cap'en, and wud play up hell sometimes wi'
the women. But he was a sportsman—niver
shot his bird sitting; and if a wuman was
pore and sorter helpless, reckoned a man stud
her friend by keeping away. He'd keep away
too, an' why shudn't he? The higher game
fell to him, dropped to his gun pretty much
as he blanked well liked. I saw the Cap'en
look at her an' frown, then look an' frown
again : 'twas the first time he had ever seen

her to take notice of. Arter a bit he fetched
his own chair and a couple o' rugs; he made
the boatswain lash the chair well out o' the
wind, and wint up to where her was standing,
took off his hat and talked sorter quiet, and
her smiled and turned back to where the chair
was, and sat down. Her acted terrible nat'rel,
as if ther wasn't nothing speshil in it one
way or t'other; but, blank yer, most women
wud have half busted therselves squirming
and showing their pints. The Cap'en he
tucked the rugs round her and wint away:
they didn't see over much of one 'nother arter
that. Sometimes he'd lend her a book or
stop and talk a bit. She took it all terrible
simple; but her fell a-thinking o' him for
all that. I know, 'cos I watched her face. I
cussed him and I cussed her, and I cussed the
line that was atween me and her, and wasn't
atween her and him. I was blanked glad
when we put inter Sydney, where men are
ekal, and I cud say to him, 'There ain't no
masters and servants in this country; you
go your way and I'll go mine.' He smiled
kind o' curious to hisself; he saw things was
pretty wrong wi' me. 'That's how you wish,

Atter,' seys he; 'but if you want a friend,'
and he took a card from his pocket wi' something scrawled on it, 'this address will find
me.' Afore I knowed wot I was arter, I up
wi' my hand and saluted; then I cussed myself for a blanked tame recruit, tore the card
across and spat on it, ther, to his face.

"Soon arter that the Cap'en went up country jackerooing,[1] but I hung about Sydney
cos she was ther. Her got a situation for the
first few months, then her left and tramped
round arter work, growing poor—cockatoo[2]
poor. Australia was a bit too noo for shabby
dressed women. One afternoon, I reckon
her was feeling terrible off colour; her took
the penny steamboat across to one o' the
islands, and I followed. I hadn't let her
know that I was still in Sydney, and I kept
aft so her shudn't spot me, and when her
landed I did my tracking careful, same as
usual. At last she sat down. 'Twas a lonesome spot,—the trees that thick all round
ther wasn't room in 'em for a dog to bark.
Her sat thinking and thinking, and I watched

[1] *Jackeroo*=a lately arrived colonist.
[2] A settler on a small farm.

her and sed to myself: 'Dick Atter, if you're the man I take yer for, you'll yard and brand that filly once for all!' But the blanked line was atween us, and I cudn't stir hand nor fut. All to a sudden it coomed to me that her was a-thinking o' the Cap'en, and wi' that the line melted like wax. I rose to my feet and coomed towards her, and her rose to her feet too, and us stood looking at one 'nother. I reckon my face was a devil's face, for her got sheet-white; but her stood there terrible quiet and proud, and the line came atween us agin, cutting me off. And when I felt that the line was atween us agin, I swore to break it and her. 'Cap'en Thursby is dead,' sed I, and her fell at my feet as one wi' the life knocked out from her——" He stopped abruptly, and wrenched apart his shirt at the throat. "Then 'twas," he said, "then 'twas . . . my brain and heart seemed to burst; but her was mine, and the line might work its will. Wot's a wuman? Wot's one blanked wuman more than another? Wot's a wuman, any way? Then I hid among the scrub, and by and bye her coomed to herself; and

wi' the consciousness comed the tears, and
her sat ther and cried 'cos her thort the
Cap'en was dead. But her didn't know
her was dead herself—her didn't know her
was dead herself. But wot's a wuman
when her's poor? If her ain't bad, her
shud be; 'tis her own fault if her ain't.
But wot's one wuman more than another?
Wot's a wuman, any way?

"An' the months went on. Her was poor,
workus poor, and I waited for her to go to hell
o' herself—I reckoned it 'ud be one then—but
her wudn't go, her wudn't go: 'twas the line
that held her back; it always stud atween her
and me. Then her got a situation, but four
months later they turned her out into the
streets; and I watched her close—I feared
she'd drown herself for horror o' wot she bore
w'in her. Then I went to a wuman that I
knowed and told the truth, word for word as
it was, and she took her in and cared for her.
Agin the winder of her room a green willer
tree rubbed its branches sorter friendly, and
she lay and stared at the willer, and stared.
Then her chil' was born; it wos a boy, fine
and healthy, and her was terrible content at

last, 'cos her had gone mad, and reckoned her was Cap'en Thursby's wife, and the chil' his chil'. I went up country and worked for 'em. Two years later I comed across the Cap'en; he spoke kind to me, but I could have killed him where he stud; but a blanky bullock did it for me—horned him in the drafting yards, bashing him up agin the postesses. They put a bullet through the beast, but the Cap'en he was most done for: he just axed me to take a message for him to the old Squire, and the blood rose up in his throat and choked the life out o' him. The manager sealed the Cap'en's watch and chain in a bit o' paper and gived it to me, and I left the station and went down south to Sydney, sorter blind stupid 'cos I cudn't fix things up in my mind one way or tother. When I got to Sydney they told me her was dying, and had axed for me. I cursed her, and said I wudn't go a-nigh her; but I walked up and down the street afore her door night and day, and at last, whether I wud or no, I entered the house and went up the stairs and stud at the door o' her room. I cudn't knock and I cudn't stir, but I stood ice-cold, wi' the sweat upon me. Then some one opened the door; she called me, and I was fo'ced to come. She was lying propped up wi' pillys, the child aside her, and death most nigh as near; the sheets was blanked coarse, and her bit o' night-shift nort to speak of, but, damn yer, it only made the breeding in her show the more. 'Atter,' she said, 'take him back to his people and tell them he is a Thursby and a gentleman,'—then she sorter tried to hold yer towards me, and fell back dead. So I took yer to the old Squire and sed wot her told me; her thought you was a Thursby—maybe her knows better now. But wot's a wuman?—wot's one wuman more than another?—wot's a wuman, any way?"

He rose from the ground. " 'Twas the line that did it," he muttered, walking across to where his horse stood. " 'Twas atween us then; 'tis atween us now," and mounting he rode away in search of the horses.

An overpowering horror of this man who was his father came to Humphrey, wiping out all other feelings. Raising himself, he crept away on his hands and knees through the rank grass; but as he struggled forward he met Atter returning, driving the horses before

him. Bullocky burst into a rough laugh.
"So yer reckoned to give me the slip," he exclaimed.

"I can't go with you," said the boy, rising
to his feet. "I'd rather be bushed outright."

"Is your little bit o' privit hell so cursed
much too much for yer?" Atter answered.
"Yer fool, yer don't know what hell is; yer
ain't niver bin in it."

"It isn't myself, it's *her*," said the boy.

"*Her!*" exclaimed Atter—"*her!* her's
mine, not yers. Ain't I gone to hell for her?
Ain't the blanked line round my neck night
and day 'cos o' her?"

"For God's sake, Atter, leave me," the boy
said.

"Leave yer," Atter answered; "no, by God,
I'll not leave yer. I did once, 'cos her told
me, but now—yer part of her, that's wot yer
are, tho' her don't belong to yer; you laid
agin her, that's wot you did, tho' her didn't
want 'ee. Ay, and by the living God, and
more than agin her; twas you her was fo'ced
to carry whether her wud or no; 'twas you
her was fo'ced to born, tho' her went mad for
it——"

"And I would like to kill you for that, you devil," cried the boy. "But I am blind, you devil,—I'm blind!"

"Kill me," repeated Atter, laughing wildly. "I can't die, that's part o' it; I'm forced to live wi' the line strangling me—half strangled, but never dead."

The man's fierce agony beat upon the boy, but he was dull and impervious to it.

"She was helpless, and a *woman*," he said.

"Do you reckon to be the first to think of that, yer fool, yer rouse-about, yer blanked jackaroo!" cried Atter fiercely. "You that have been playing the busted fine gentleman all your life, how long have yer bin in hell 'cos o' her tears, 'cos o' her pain? Go and git they sheep's eyes o' yers put right; start crying on yer own account, and leave her to me."

He slung himself to the ground as he spoke, caught and saddled the other horses, cording the swag across the pack-saddle.

"Come," he said to the boy, "here's yer stirrup——"

"I'll not go with you," cried Humphrey, with growing excitement. "Aren't you content with what you have done? Do you want to drive me mad too?"

"By the living Gawd, I'll make yer come," Bullocky answered, taking a quick step towards the boy. Then the passion died out of his face, and, stopping short, "Mad," he exclaimed in an altered voice—"mad—'twas her I sent mad; yer I blinded. Mother and son; mother and son."

The boy shuddered. "No power on earth will make me acknowledge myself your son," he said. "It can't be true; it can't be true."

"'Tis sorter blanked true all the same," Atter answered slowly—"sorter blanked tarnation true."

There was a sound of approaching footsteps, and four police troopers closed in upon them.

"Hands up, Bullocky, or we'll fire," they said, levelling revolvers.

Atter made no effort to escape, but stood stone-still, staring at his son's face, with its expression of sudden joy, of great elation.

CHAPTER III

Atter was tried at the Sydney Assizes for manslaughter (the police trooper had died), and sentenced to three years' hard labour. He accepted the sentence with callous indifference; no vision of the murdered trooper haunted him; between him and the memory of other misdeeds there stood a dead woman, and into his fierce, passionate heart had come a fierce, passionate need of her forgiveness. Longing and dumb—dumb with the dumbness of the beasts of the field, dumb even to himself—he could not analyse his own terrible yearning. Remorse, like cancer, spread fibrous hands upon his life and ate its slow way into his heart; yet he did not realise what ailed him, and, racked by conscience, scarce understood that he had sinned. Ill, dying, he toiled with the unceasing energy of a man who would out-toil his own thoughts. Work forbidden him, confined to the hospital, he wept like a child, and lay with his face turned towards the ward door, as if he

5

waited for the entry of some bringer of healing.   The prison chaplain, knowing the man
to be dying, and struck by the expression of
acute misery on the gaunt face, asked if there
was any person that he desired to see.

" Is there some one," he asked gently,
" whose forgiveness would make you hap-
pier ? "

" Forgiveness ! " repeated Atter, glancing
at him in astonishment—" wot the blanky
blank should I want with forgiveness ; I ain't
done nothing to be ashamed of.   I've alles
acted the man."

The chaplain smiled, but made no further
suggestion, and Atter fell back again to staring at the closed door.   He did not know
whose face it was that he waited for with
such an intensity of yearning ; but one day
the chaplain entered, and with him was Humphrey, and when Atter's eyes fell upon his
son there came to him a sudden great elation.

" I sorter thought yer wud come," he exclaimed.   " I sorter thought it ; I sorter
thought it."

Humphrey stumbled forward till within
a few paces of the bed, and stood stock-still,

his terrible repulsion of the man seeming to bind him hand and foot. The chaplain went out, leaving them alone.

"I've bin reckoning things out," continued Atter, "reckoning things out a bit; but I've lost the hang o' 'em, yer came so blanked sudden. I sorter thought yer wud come, tho'; sorter thought it. They blanked eyes o' yers ain't bin after healing, I see; well, I sorter reckoned they wudn't, sorter reckoned they wudn't. Things have gone on the cross wi' me iver since I played on the cross wi' her, and her was nothing but a blanked wuman, and wot's a wuman, any way?"

Humphrey shuddered. "Atter," he said, rushing into speech to avoid the greater horror of listening, "I've been a mucker myself since we parted. I speculated with some money of —of—my grandfather's—of—of—, I mean— the Squire's; he sent it to me under the impression that I was his grandson—you understand,—well, I speculated with the money."

Atter's face lit up. "Yer lost it, and comed to me sorter reckoning I wud help yer make it good. Ay, I know the brand!"

The blood rushed up to the boy's forehead. "No," he answered—"no, no; not for *that*."

But Atter did not heed him, into his eyes had come an expression of mighty triumph. "Wot's bred in the bone 'ull come out in the flesh," he cried. "'Twas my blood in yer that forced 'ee to do it. Y'are my son; yer ain't no blanked Thursby. Didn't I tell yer yer wasn't no blanked Thursby; y'are my son and hers, my son and hers."

As the words fell on Humphrey's ears he staggered forward and clutched at the iron bedstead for support, missed it, and fell across the man's feet. Atter stretched out his great, coarse, trembling hands towards his son.

"My oath," he said, "ye're blind, stone-blind. I didn't reckon on yer being stone-blind; I didn't sorter reckon on yer being stone-blind."

"Stone-blind!" repeated the boy, "stone-blind!"

Atter stared down on him in silence; the silence swelled, the agony in the man's heart fighting with it; at last he spoke. "Go back along 'ome to 'em," he said, "they care for yer. Go back and be a blanked Thursby; I'll never blab on yer. Go and be a blanked gintleman, they'll never know; they'll be glad to see yer; they'll nuss yer; yer'll be at 'ome ther, you ain't niver bin easy 'long o' me."

"Atter, Atter," sobbed the boy, "I'm stone-blind; the doctor told me there was no hope."

"Go back to 'em, then," Atter answered. "Wot's the good o' yer staying here? Yer can't play no blanked concertina; yer can't go on the wallaby wi' a blanked dawg and a piece of string."

The boy's shoulders shook with sobs, but he made no answer.

"Go back to 'em," harped Atter. "Yer ain't built for nort else; yer was alles blanked tarnation shook on being a busted gintleman; go back and *be* one, then—I'll never blab on 'ee."

"You don't understand," said Humphrey.

"But yer *are* shook on being a gintleman."

"Yes."

"Ah!"—triumphantly, "thet's her blood in 'ee. 'Twas mine thet made yer a thief; hers wud make 'ee a gintleman; my son and hers, my son and hers,"—again his face glowed.

There was a long silence,—then the boy raised his blind eyes to Atter's face.

"It's no use," he said, "I can't go back; it's too late."

"Why too late?"

"I've told them the truth. It *is* the truth?" he added—with a wild hope that Atter might even yet contradict his former statement.

"Ay, God's truth."

"I've told them, then."

"You've told 'em?—told the old Squire? Yer have owned up—owned to the brand? Yer sed—I was yer—father?"

"Yes."

Into Atter's hard, brutal face there came an expression of gladness, of great radiance; suddenly his expression changed. "Yer ain't so blanked set on being a gintleman arter all," he said.

The boy winced. "Clinging to a name that was not mine would not make me a gentleman," he answered.

"If nobody knowed, 'twud."

"But I should know."

"Wot blanked difference wud that make?"

"Atter," said the boy, "you don't understand."

"Maybe I don't; 'tis a busted ring-tailed consarn, any way. So yer are going to let the gintleman business slide," he continued in a regretful voice.

His son was silent, the colour coming and going in his face. "No," he said, half to himself, "I don't think so."

"Yer'll go back to 'em then, and ask 'em not to peach on 'ee?"

"No."

"Stay here?"

"Yes."

"Wot—and play a blanked concertina!"

"Something of the sort."

"Thet ain't being a gintleman."

Humphrey raised his blind eyes towards the light. "The Squire said once," he exclaimed, "that as long as a man is a man, he, for one, wouldn't ask more of him."

"But," replied Atter, "that's a pore tale; I've bin a gintleman myself on that showing."

"It's no poor thing to keep one's record clean," the boy answered; "I haven't, but

——" he was silent a moment. "It doesn't matter then," he continued, "how much one fails in other things, one need not fear to look any man in the face."

"*Thet* a gintleman!" exclaimed Atter derisively. "Why, blank yer, I niver was afeared to look no blamed joker between the eyes; but then the Squire was a musclely man hisself."

Humphrey made no comment, and after a while Atter continued in a dull, monotonous voice, as if talking aloud to himself: "I niver was afeared of no man living nor dead, niver; and niver had no cause to be ashamed o' not acting the man; her and the line near got the best o' me once; but I broke 'em, her and the line togither; no man can throw it at me that I didn't break 'em: I broke 'em, and—I broke meself a-breaking 'em; but no man can throw it at me that I didn't break 'em first. No; as I sed afore, I ain't done nothing to be ashamed of, and ther's on'y two thet I knows on thet I wud like to make things right with: one wos her; I cud niver make things right wi' her, 'cos her sorter got away from me, sorter kept outside; wint mad, and sorter

kept outside. Ther was on'y her and one
other, the lad her borned—her son and mine,
her son and mine."

He stopped speaking, and the boy, staring
with blind eyes into a dark world, made no
answer.

"It's a queer thing," continued Atter, " a
queer ring-tailed thing. I hadn't sorter speshil wanted to work her no harm—hadn't
sorter speshil wanted to hurt 'em, either o'
'em ; but I sent her mad, I blinded him—
mother and son, mother and son."

"You didn't mean to blind me," Humphrey
answered huskily.

"I hadn't no sorter speshil wish—no sorter
speshil wish."

"I shall pull through all right," said Humphrey. " I'm not beaten yet."

"Yer ain't beaten yit," Atter answered,
" but yer won't niver make things right wi'
me."

"Atter," exclaimed the boy, "I could if it
weren't for her."

"Her," repeated Atter, and his voice was
infinitely sad—"her, her, her ; her comed
atween me and herself, her comes atween me

and her son; her was niver mine tho' I held
her in my arms; and when I reckoned to
have her body and soul, her stud away from
me—her stud away from me."

"Atter, Atter," said the boy, "Atter,
Atter."

"Ay, Atter, Atter," the man repeated,
"Atter, Atter; Atter 'twas wi' yer from the
fust, Atter 'twill be wi' yer to the end."

"Father," said the boy huskily.

In hesitation the words came stuttering
forth. Atter's heart stopped a beat to listen,
and then slammed back against his ribs, the
whole man rocking in the unreality of his own
happiness. He put out his hands in trembling hesitation, then, conquered by all-
mastering desire, drew the boy to him, up
against his breast; and within the breast his
heart clanged and throbbed as some impris-
oned engine. Gripped close in his father's
arms, inert from pity, sundered from him by
repulsion, the son's mind groped in agonising
longing for some link that should be an
ennobling bond of union.

"Father," he said, "shall we not lead
straighter lives because of *her*?"

The great engine within Atter's breast strained more wildly against its imprison-ment.

"Her cudn't change me when her was alive ; her'll never do it now her's dead," he answered. "No, no, I'll bide as I am : when my time comes for loosing ropes and slipping the stock-yard rails, I reckon hell 'ull about do me—a place where a man can curse free and fight for his own, come God, come devil,"— and so saying, his heart burst bonds, his grip on his son relaxed, and with a sob he fell back dead.

PART III

HUMPHREY, SON OF ATTER

CHAPTER I

IT was late afternoon; Atter had been buried in the prison graveyard, and Humphrey, refusing the chaplain's offer of a temporary home, returned to his lodgings. They were ill-furnished rooms in a mean street, but the rent was more than he could afford, and he decided that he must leave them. On the mantelpiece in the sitting-room was an unopened telegram. Searching with his long, awkward fingers, Humphrey found and held the telegram a moment in his hand before tearing it slowly into bits,—then he left the room and the house.

He crossed the street, taking short, undecided steps,—resenting as ignominious the necessity which obliged him to tap with his

stick each foot of the ground in advance,—
and, wandering on, turned at last into a blind
alley in one of the poorest quarters of the
town. Seated close to a doorstep, a short,
deep-chested man was mending the broken
ribs of a still more broken umbrella, whistling over his work with such evident satisfaction that Humphrey could not help sharing in
the enjoyment.

"Good day," said the man; "I reckon, by
the sound of your stick, you're blind yirself."

"Were you whistling just now?" asked
Humphrey in reply.

"I was so."

"Well, I should never have imagined that
you were blind."

"And why not?" said the man; "I ain't
heard as blindness puts a shut on whistling."

Humphrey leant up against the wall of the
house; the stick slipping from his hand compelled him to grovel along the none too clean
street in search of it, and when, the stick regained, he once more resumed his position, his
face burnt with anger and tears of shame
stood in his eyes.

"Great heavens!" he exclaimed, "how I

hate being compelled to tap my way along with a stick."

"Well," said the man, "the stick was put in the world to be o' some use, I reckon, the same as the rest o' us; but then," he added, "maybe you're noo to it,—a stick wants knowing the same as a man. I fell out with my little gidea a mint o' times before us took to one another comfortable, and now us is as thick as thieves."

Humphrey smiled. "How long have you been blind?" he asked.

"A matter o' twenty years."

"Twenty years!"

"Well," replied the man, "you'll be saying the like some day, I reckon."

Humphrey turned the subject with a shudder. "What are you working at?" he said.

"Mending ginghams, and a mighty pore trade it is, by the same token."

"I wonder you don't hang yourself."

"Wot good wud that do, wi' the Missus slaving herself to the bone as 'tis?"

"You have a wife dependent on you?"

"Well," replied the man, with a slow smile,

"us puts it that way, though maybe the truth is t'other end about."

Humphrey was silent a moment, he won·dered at the man acknowledging so lightly a galling dependence.

"How did you become blind?" he asked at length. "Was it an accident?"

"Yes; one of they things that there ain't no speshil reason why they should happen, but happen they does. I was doing a job o' fencing up Cooramingle way; 'twas summer, and powerful hot by the same token ; I had sandy blight tarnation bad—sorter feel as if yer eyes was full of red-hot grit; termaters is the best thing, cut 'em in half and reg'lar soak your eyes in the squash; but there wasn't no termaters, so I had to blamed well do without 'em. Jim Day, the chap I was working 'long with, a good·hearted jumbuck but a reg'lar mutton-head, let on to me that he had some doctor's stuff that wud put a set on the blight smart enough. I hadn't no great trust in Jim's cures, but my eyes was that bad I thort they couldn't be much wuss, so I ses to him, 'Jim, bring out that healing o' nations o' a cure o' yirs;' so he brought it out, powerful pleased,—a better-hearted chap there never was. 'You must go the whole hog, Joe,' he ses; 'half measures ain't no manner o' use ; set to, and souse yir eyes in it, same as if they was afire. My oath ! but they look bad ! "

" 'Holy Moses ! but this stuff o' yirs is powerful strong, Jim,' I ses ; 'twas burning fair to scorch my eyes out.

" ' It's got a decent opinion o' itself,' ses he.

" ' Well,' I ses, ' it fair needs to, for I much misdoubt if 'twill find another to speak for it, less 'tis a salamander.'

" ' Be they easing a bit now ? ' ses Jim.

" I lifted up my head. ' Jim,' I ses, ' have I any eyes left, for, by all the snakes, I feel the same as if they was burnt clean out ! '

" ' Strike me dead ! ' ses Jim, ' but I think they're healing slow.'

" ' You ain't got hold of the wrong stuff ? ' ses I.

" ' I'll take another look at the bottle,' ses he. ' Why, 'tis Barty's Patent Sciatica Singe-ger, by all the crawling sons o' a bullock ! ' he cried.

" ' Well,' ses I, ' it's patented me sure

enough ; ' and so it had, licked the sight out
o' my eyes as clean as a cat a cream-jug.
Holy Moses ! but I was fair mad wi' Jim at
the time, but now there ain't one day in seven
that I notices there's anything wrong with
my eyes at all."

" Can a man get as used to being blind as
that ? "

" Blind ain't the right name for it. You
sees less of the outside of a pussen's head,
but you learns a deal more wot goes on
inside o' it; and, 'pon my sam, you gains
by the change, tho' I allow 'tis tarnation
hard to swaller. Jest you wait till you've
bin blind as long as I have, and, mark me,
you'll say the same."

Humphrey was silent; the colour came and
went in his face. " Is your work difficult? "
he asked at last.

" No; any mug could learn it."

" Well "—hurriedly—" take me as a pupil
—an apprentice. I mean—I—I wish you
would."

" In the umbrella trade? What's bin your
line so far? " the man asked in an astonished
voice.

6

The blood rushed back into Humphrey's face. "I have never done much worth the doing, I'm afraid," he answered.

"How long have you bin blind?"

"Six months."

"You haven't got the feel o' your fingers yit, then?"

"No; I muff things rather."

"Ain't you got no friends?"

"I hate being dependent."

"That's it, is it?"

"I could pay for my food and lodging for the first few months," Humphrey pleaded.

A woman walked with heavy tread from the interior of the house and joined them.

"Don't you be after doing nothing rash, Joe," she exclaimed in a harsh, high-pitched tone. "The young man's a step above us; he's stood behind counters—I can see that by the look of his hands."

"I never stood behind a counter in my life!" spluttered Humphrey indignantly.

"Then you've bin after no good, that's all I can say," rejoined the woman. "Them hands speaks for thirselves: they look, for all the

world, the same as William Splinter's hands
did after he comed out o' jail."

"Hush, mother! the young chap's blind,"
Joe interposed soothingly. "You needn't
pay no manner o' attention to what she ses,"
he continued, turning to Humphrey; "her
ain't dipped in alum farther than the tongue."

Humphrey laughed a little awkwardly,
and the woman cast a quick glance at him
and smiled to herself.

"Now go along in, mother, and bring us
a cup o' tea," said Joe, and his wife returned
once more to the kitchen. "I used to give
her the strap one time," he continued, lower-
ing his voice; "that was when I could see,
the same as the rest. Now the strap hangs
on the nail aside the dresser, and I find her
acts a sight more reasonable wi'out it. A
woman is a queer thing—more heart than
sense; but the sense her has carries her tarnation far on the right road."

As he spoke his wife called them into the
house to tea, and Humphrey, drawing his
chair forward to the little table, felt strangely content.

"How good your bread and butter tastes!"

he said. " I do wish you would let me work under you."

Joe laughed. " Holy Moses ! " he exclaimed, " but that's an uncommon rum reason for taking to a trade—eh, mother ? "

The woman's somewhat hard face softened into a smile. " Bread and butter is bread and butter," she answered sententiously.

" Take me on trial," urged Humphrey, pressing his advantage ; " I shouldn't be any expense to you."

" What do you say, mother ? " Joe asked, and the boy waited with keen anxiety for the answer. He had a sudden longing to be near this man, who was blind, and whom he suspected of being happy.

The woman's eyes rested a moment on him with a half-amused, half-pitying expression. " Oh," she answered, " let him come ; 'tis only a fad. 'Twon't last long any way."

" Not a fad, but a bargain ! " exclaimed Humphrey, stretching his hand across the table towards her. " Shake hands on it, and wish me every success in the umbrella trade."

The woman took the proffered hand in her crinkly red one a little awkwardly. " Come right up-stairs and look at your room first along," she said. "As like as not the bed won't suit 'ee. 'Tis nought but a straw mattress; but it's clean, I'll lay to that."

"Oh, bother the bed!" exclaimed Humphrey. "Haven't I tasted the bread and butter?"

"Don't try and come over me with yer soft sawder," replied the woman in a severe voice. "When a bed is hills and dales, I niver heard as bread and butter 'ud mend it."

Humphrey rose and stumbled up the steep staircase.

"Now," she exclaimed, as they entered the attic, "let me see you take the feel o' the room."

Reddening, the boy crossed the attic, hands extended, hitting his shins against the poor bits of furniture.

"Stay right where you are," said the woman peremptorily. He halted. "Now, find the door," she continued. But he failed to do so, knocking the little painted washstand till the jug rang in the basin.

"Ah!" she exclaimed, "you'll never be a patch on Joe."

Humphrey rubbed his knees. "I very much doubt if I shall," he answered, laughing. But the woman did not smile in return; in her eyes the subject was too serious for smiles. Leading him across the room, she told him to feel the mattress; and he did so half-heartedly.

"Surely that is mignonette I smell," he exclaimed, brightening.

Her face relaxed. "We always had some in the Old Country, and me and Joe thought 'twud be a pore thing if us cudn't have some here," she answered.

"You're English!" he exclaimed, adding impulsively, "aren't you, aren't you homesick—sometimes, I mean?"

She picked a dead leaf off the mignonette. "Ah, whiles," she answered slowly; "but ther, as I've said many a time, 'life's life.'"

Humphrey was silent; at last he spoke, changing the subject. "Tell me about the board," he said. "Would a pound a-week be right?"

"Why, bless us," she answered, "half that is more than enough, and I'd mend and wash 'ee for the same."

"Am I to have bread and butter every day as good as I had this afternoon?" he asked, smiling.

She glanced at him with quick suspicion; but his boyish face with its look of suffering disarmed her.

"Ah," she said, "you're a soft-tongued one, you are."

"You'll forgive me for not having stood behind counters or been in jail?" he asked.

"I've known good men who have done both," she said.

"But we are friends," he urged: his smile was whimsical, but there was almost entreaty in his voice. He had seated himself at the head of the bed opposite her. She looked a moment at his thin white face before answering.

"I shall mother 'ee my own way," she said.

Humphrey returned to his lodgings full of thought but very elate. His landlady met him in the hall. "A letter, sir," she said; "would you like me to read it to you?" she added, with an uncurbed curiosity that jarred upon the boy.

"No, no," he replied, holding out his hand for the letter.

" From England," she continued, still retaining her hold of it.

" Ah ! "

" Post-mark Thursby,—a queer, angular handwriting, something like the herring-bone stitch."

" My grandfather's," exclaimed Humphrey below his breath.

" Best let me read it to you, sir."

" No, thanks," he answered, his fingers closing on the letter. "I'm not particularly interested in the contents."

" Who knows but it's a death and a fortune," she said, striving to whet his curiosity.

Humphrey took the letter from her with a gentle force, and, entering his room, shut the door upon the prying woman. Stumbling into a chair the boy sank his face in his hands. "Blind, blind, blind," he sobbed,— " blind, blind, blind,—I can't read it myself; I couldn't stand her prying eyes. I shall never know what he thinks; I shall never know what he thinks."

Long he sat staring down on the letter with sightless eyes; the sun sank; the woman entered with a lamp.

" I've brought you a lamp, sir," she said ; "maybe it will be welcome to you."

He laughed brokenly. " Yes," he answered, " a little light, a little light." Then he put the unopened letter in his pocket and went out.

CHAPTER II

The next week Humphrey left his lodgings and went to live with Joe and his wife. Some days later he was seated with an old disreputable umbrella that Joe had given him to repair on his knees; but the only point about the umbrella of which he felt complete assurance was its offensive smell.

" Joe," he said, " where did you pick up this umbrella ? "

" So long ago I can't remember," the man answered. " It's the one I learned the trade on. What's the matter with it ? "

" Smell it."

" Don't notice nothing particular," Joe replied, handing it back. " Laid in a drain, I spose."

Humphrey dropped the umbrella, and its

ancient ribs were still clattering protestingly against the stone floor when the woman, entering the kitchen, crossed to where he sat with depression heavy upon him.

" If your room ain't a reglar disgrace, I don't know what is," she exclaimed. " Everything left sixes and sevens, as if I hadn't enough to do looking after a blind husband without trapesing round after you all day long. Why, it's my firm belief you've stud in that basin, which ain't big enough to hold a six months' old baby, and had a bath all round it; the whole room is fair swimming wi' water, and that's not counting the things that be splashing about by theirselves—a coat here, a shirt there, and goodness knows what else anywhere and everywhere ! Now, jest you march straight up-stairs this very instant and mop up ivery drop o' that watter yirself."

Humphrey stumbled to his feet, red in the face, impelled by a strong desire to take flight before the woman's angry tongue.

" Take the cloth right along up wi' you," the woman continued, thrusting a heavy moist floor-cloth into his reluctant hands,

"and don't you dare show your face down
here till that room is fit to be seen!"

"You mustn't be too hard on him, mother,"
interposed Joe soothingly, as the door of
Humphrey's attic closed with a bang. "I
reckon that life 'long o' us comes fair strange
to him."

"'Twas his own free will that he came
here, nobody axed him," replied the angry
woman; "but as like as not he'll be putting
his bit o' things together at this very minnit,
and a good riddance too."

"No, no, mother, you don't mean that,"
her husband answered. "Besides, the poor
chap's blind."

"And ain't you blind yourself?" she replied indignantly. "I've niver heard you ax
no speshil grace a-cos o' it."

"Maybe I hadn't so much to lose as him."

"Niver you tell me that your sight ain't as
much vally as his. He niver used his eyes to
look about him when he had 'em, or he wudn't
be so blind as he is."

"Well," said Joe, "I reckon he's a gintleman, and ain't bin used to taking notice."

"Ay, gintleman," the woman answered;

"he's got the vices o' one any way—wot wi'
wasting good victuals and swamping the
place; but there, gintleman or no, he's got to
learn the same as the rest.   Life's life for high
and low."

"Maybe, mother, but then steamed sticks
straighten a mint better taken gradual than
fo'ced all to once."

"You was always a bit of a soft, Joe," answered his wife, busying herself pouring out
a cup of tea.   Placing it beside him, she
fetched another cup from the dresser, filled it
with tea—dark in colour, bitter in taste—
and, adding much brown sugar, as a sign of
reconciliation, she   climbed   up-stairs   and
opened the door of Humphrey's room.   The
attic presented a deplorable spectacle: water
stood in pools on the unplaned boards, and
Humphrey, after giving an ineffectual swab,
had thrown the cloth out of the window.   A
hasty glance into the garden revealed it to the
woman lying on Joe's freshly-washed linen.
Her anger kindled anew at the sight; but,
turning, she saw the boy seated in so forlorn
an attitude, and with so forlorn an expression
on his face, that though it went to her heart

not to speak her mind, she put the cup of tea
down on the chest of drawers and left the
room in silence.

Coming back later she found Humphrey
had rubbed the floor dry with one of his
shirts.

"Bless us, did you iver see the like o'
that!" she exclaimed, dropping her hands
despairingly on to her apron. "A four-years-
old chile wud have known better; but there,"
she continued, stemming back her indignation,
"let the floor alone, do, and drink your tea—
it's stone cold by this time."

He took the cup from her. "I am afraid
I am an awful nuisance to you," he said.

"You ain't niver bin taught better," she
answered. "I warrant you've bin fine and
spoiled in your time; but then the Almighty
seed for Hisself that you needed a dressing,
or He would never have brought 'ee to the
pass He has."

Putting the cup down, the boy turned away
with a sort of half sob, and the woman's face
softened.

"Ah, lad, us have all got to go through
wi' it," she said. "Life's life."

"I'm an awful fool," he said, straightening his back; "it's only the being blind."

"Poor lad!" said the woman, "poor lad!"

"Joe is a fine fellow," exclaimed the boy, enviously.

"He's larned," she answered, "he's larned."

"It seems so desperately hard," said the boy, "anything but blindness—anything in the whole world but that."

"Us ain't got the choosing of our own burdens; us must fit 'em to our backs as best us can," she answered.

Turning to her he held out his hands. "Will you have patience with me while I learn?" he asked.

"I shall mother 'ee my own way," she answered.

"Mother is a comforting word," said Humphrey, smiling.

"Oh, you're a soft-tongued one, you are," she answered.

The days passed slowly away, and little by little Humphrey found what Joe called "the feel o' his fingers." Other things he learned of greater value; unperceived by himself his views of life were altering, and he realised dimly that a position of dependence might still be compatible with self-respect. Perhaps he was able to look at the subject with less bias, because he could now earn sufficient to support himself; and, having escaped being dependent, recognised that another might be justified in submitting to so galling a position. One afternoon he was seated at work beside his blind friend; the woman was ironing clothes, and the bang, bang of her hot iron on the clean linen resounded monotonously through the small kitchen. After a while Joe, who had let his work fall on his knees, turned to her.

"Mother," he said, "my throat has been fine and sore these last weeks; I reckon that one of your poultices might do it a good turn."

"Now that's just like you, Joe, being so long a-mentioning it," she answered in a tart voice.

"Well, I thought 'twud better itself; but 'tis rare and contrary," he replied, sipping some cold tea from a pannikin beside him.

The woman watched him, but made no remark.

"Why not get a doctor to look at it?" suggested Humphrey.

"Oh, it takes a pound o' money to git a penn'orth o' sense out o' them," Joe replied, draining the pannikin to the dregs. His wife rose and quietly refilled the tin mug with tea.

"I have a friend you can consult for noth·ing, if you like," rejoined Humphrey; "and a clever fellow too."

"Ay," said the woman, "do 'ee go up and see the gintleman. I ain't no friend to sore throats."

Joe did not answer for a moment, and sighed rather weariedly. "Well," he ex·claimed at last, "maybe I will."

On the examination taking place, the doctor refused to give an opinion, asking him to come back again on the following day. Returning home after the second consultation, his wife met him at the door.

"What did the gintleman say?" she in·quired anxiously.

"Why, there was three of 'em there this arternoon," he answered, smiling, "and it took the whole busted lot jest to tell me I wasn't on no account to smoke."

"Didn't they say no more than that, Joe?"

"Not a blamed word."

"Bless us!" exclaimed his wife, "but doctors git their larning hard. Where's the lad?" she continued, after a pause.

"Oh, he stayed on there to dinner."

"Why, he had his dinner at twelve o'clock before he went away."

"Oh," said Joe, seating himself and stretching out his legs, "'tis a gintleman's meal—meat-tea, with the tea left out."

"Thank the Lord I've never been asked to fathom such heathenish meals as they," his wife exclaimed piously.

Joe dropped his head between his hands. "I'm powerful thirsty, mother," he said. "My throat burns that bad I reckon sometimes that I can 'most hear it fizz."

The woman turned towards the fire. "The kettle's jest on the boil," she answered; "I'll make yer a drop o' tea. 'Tis a queer thing," she added after a pause, "that jest the leaving off o' smoking shud cure 'ee; but there, I was niver no friend to terbacca."

When the doctors had departed, Humphrey joined his friend in the smoking-room. He

7

had been one of the doctors at the hospital where Humphrey had undergone treatment, and had taken a liking for the boy; but Humphrey kept apart from him, confiding his troubles to no one.

"What was the result of the consultation?" asked Humphrey.

The doctor rolled a cigarette neatly between his fingers before answering. "The man has cancer in the throat," he replied at length.

Humphrey's face contracted. "Is the case hopeless?" he exclaimed.

"Quite; it means——"

"What?"

"Loss of voice first, starvation afterwards."

The boy pushed his chair violently back. "What a hell of suffering this world is!" he exclaimed.

The doctor made no comment.

"Did you tell him?" Humphrey continued after a pause.

"No; I thought it might be advisable for you to break the truth to his wife, and let her tell him."

"Don't ask me to do *that*," protested the boy passionately.

"It would be the kinder way of breaking the truth to him."

Humphrey stumbled up from his chair, crossed the room, and stood with his back to his friend. "How, how, how," he exclaimed, "could I tell her such a terrible truth as that?"

"I cannot answer you," said the doctor. "My lad," he continued after a moment, rising and laying his hand on Humphrey's shoulder, "some one must tell her."

"She has been so awfully good to me," protested the boy again.

"Well, and isn't that—? eh?——"

"I understand what you mean," said Humphrey. "Damn it, man, I see what you mean; I'll—I'll tell her."

The next afternoon Joe was absent; his wife sat sewing at the little table by the window, and Humphrey, putting down the umbrella he had been recovering, came and stood beside her.

"Mother," he said (he had taken to calling her mother), "I have something to tell you."

"Well, lad," she answered, "say on."

A great knob rose in his throat. "It's about Joe's illness," he said.

She dropped her work, and looking up at him, " Yer ain't going to tell me nothing bad o' it ? " she exclaimed anxiously.

He knelt down and put his arms round her. "Oh, mother ! " he answered, "it is the old terrible thing, life's life."

She gave a little abrupt, cry. " He ain't to be took from me; it ain't that ? " she said, "it ain't that ? "

Humphrey looked at her, but answered nothing ; she turned from him and dropping her head on the table, "My pore Joe," she said, "my pore Joe." After a while she asked suddenly, "What illness is it ? "

Drawing a quick, painful breath, Humphrey answered, " Cancer in the throat."

"Oh, 'tis cruel, cruel," she cried, "and he with such a throat for trills. There ain't his ekal for singing ' Banks and braes.' "

The boy made no answer.

"I know what 'tis," she continued; "I've heard tell o' it before; twenty years he's bin blind, now he's to be dumb, then starved. Oh, Joe, my pore Joe, the Almighty must have been fair mazed wi' the joys o' heaven when He reckoned such suffering nought compared to it." She dropped her head once more upon the table and sobbed. At last she lifted up her face, the rugged lines on it a little softened.

"He'll be able to take his drop o' tea to the end," she said. "Maybe the Almighty thought on that when He made him look unkind on victuals."

In the silence that ensued the distant tapping of Joe's stick on the pavement became audible. "There he comes," exclaimed the woman, "there he comes." Humphrey put his arms round her and gave her a big, boyish hug. "Dear mother," he said, "dear mother;" then he went out and left the husband and wife alone.

Joe seemed very tired; he sat on the worn, shiny chair, the palms of his hands upon his knees. The woman rose and poured him out a cup of tea from the little brown teapot that always stood upon the hob.

"You've bin a long time," she said. "Did you buy they withies?"

"No," he answered; "they was touched

wi' the rot, so I went on as far as the Heads
and laid down on the grass a bit; 'tis a long
while since I've heard the sound o' the sea."

"Yer was alles fond o' the sea and the
grass, Joe."

"Ther's a blamed lot o' nater in 'em," he
answered; "but they alles sets me thinking
o' the Old Country. I reckons us won't set
eyes on the Old Country again, mother?"

She did not answer.

"You've bin a good wife to me," he said.

"Nought to speak of," she answered, her
voice breaking.

"Ay, but you have," he said. "I was
reckoning to myself this arternoon 'twas a
poor day when I put the strap to yer."

"It hangs on the nail now," she exclaimed,
half to herself.

"Ay, and let it."

"I've spoke my mind to the rest o' 'em,
but you was alles my master, Joe," she said.

"There ain't no disputing I've layed it into
'ee at times," he answered, with a half smile.

"I've slept the easier for it. I've known
your mind when maybe I shud niver have
known my own."

"Well, well," he exclaimed, "they days be done."

She turned away, and taking up the loaf began cutting the bread. "I've nought but a bit o' dripping for 'ee to-day," she said; "they ain't paid me for the washing yet along, and I was niver no friend to debt."

"You're right there, mother," he answered; "and I likes a bit o' dripping turn about."

"There have bin times when us cudn't git either," she said.

"Yes," he replied, smiling across at her— "us have bin fo'ced to fare scanty now and agin; but ther, hard times haven't hurt us."

"You was alles a well-plucked un, Joe," she said.

"Us fared and fared alike, mother, and I reckon, God willing, us 'ull do it till the end."

"Ay, God willing," she said, and her voice broke.

"Wot's come to 'ee, mother?"

"Joe, Joe," she answered, putting her arms around his neck, "God ain't willing. 'Tis just that; 'tis just that."

"Wot makes 'ee take on so?" he asked

anxiously. "Yer ain't kept it from me that you're ill?"

She drew him close to her. "Oh, Joe!" she exclaimed, "'tis yerself that is sicker than you reckon."

He did not answer, but putting up his hand stroked her faded hair : the tears coursed down her red freckled face, God wot she was ugly enough; but she had a heart to love with, and what greater gift has He given to man or woman yet?—what greater, though the symbol be a crown of Thorns, a Cross, and the steep steps of Calvary?

"Ay, mother," he exclaimed at last, " ain't us alles said as how life was life?"

"Life's life," she answered; "but oh, Joe, lad, 'tis hard to live it."

CHAPTER III

The grisly disease that had attacked the blind man pursued its course with startling rapidity ; and, favoured by the climate, drove its victim along the road to death at a right merry pace, so that he had reached his destination before he had half realised the direc-

tion in which he had been hurried. Joe dead,
his former customers found a passable make-
shift in Humphrey; they grumbled, paid less,
but gave him plenty of employment. This
was all that he needed from them, caring
little for their grumbling, for his thoughts
were full of other matters. Seated on the
broken doorstep, repairing the ribs of some
neighbour's broken gingham, his heart would
swell with homesickness, and a terrible longing for the people he had known and loved in
childhood take possession of him. Then the
umbrella would drop from his hand, and his
blind eyes fill with visions of his English
home; the crude street noises around him
would hush themselves, and the lop-lop of the
river, as it humped its way over brown peb-
bles, become audible: he watched it wind
through the Thursby meadows where the big
elms lolled and sunned themselves, past the
gorse-covered hills, and the shuffling woods in
their spring coat of beech-green. He saw again
the long green alleys of the Chase, played in
its old-world gardens, where old-world flowers
dozed with drooping heads as if dog-tired of
blooming. Watching, the boy's heart would

swell with homesickness, and he would creep
up-stairs to the little attic, fling himself upon
the bed, and sob like the fool that he was.
The woman marked the traces of tears on his
face, but made no comment; and the days
crept on, each much as the other. Humphrey
had bought a small book of Devonshire stories, and when the evenings came and the
woman had put away her work, she would sit
upright in the wooden arm-chair and read to
him from the pages of the book, monotonously
and with much labour, and he would sit on
the floor at her feet, his head resting against
her knee. She never commented on the stories.
They were descriptive of rustic life in Devonshire, and one day Humphrey asked for her
opinion of them.

"The book has a fine cover of its own," she
said; "but there, I reckoned when you laid
out your money on such things you wud have
liked to walk in higher life. I ain't come
across no dook, though I've read each page
careful."

"Why a duke, mother?"

"There ain't nothing scanty about a dook,"
she answered. "Set him where you will, he

makes the page look full. I've alles held it a
queer thing that, thinking of dooks as I do,
the Almighty has never seen fit to throw us
together; but ther, that's life all over, the
man as admires 'ee most is fate sure to miss
'ee by the turn of a street."

Into Humphrey's face there came a mingled
expression of amused, delighted affection. He
rose from his chair and put his arms round
the old woman.

"You are worth all the dukes and duch-
esses put together," he said. "If ever I
could write a book, it would be about
you."

"Oh, you're a soft-tongued one, *you* are,"
she answered, smiling. He lifted her crinkled
red hand and put it tenderly to his lips.

"Mother," he said, "you suspect flattery
in everything."

"Bless the boy," she exclaimed, "you've
tored the pocket o' your coat 'most clean out,
so jest you take it off and I'll put a stitch in
it at once. "Why," she continued a moment
later, "if you ain't got three letters from the
Old Country in yer pocket, and niver so much
as broke the seal o' one o' them!"

Humphrey flushed heavily, but made no answer.

"Lad," said the old woman, in a serious voice, "I much misdoubt if you have acted fair to them that loves yer."

"I couldn't read the letters myself, and I couldn't endure the thought of an outsider reading them," protested Humphrey.

She shook her head. "You larn hard, lad," she said.

"Mother, *you* read them," he answered at last.

Searching in her work-basket, she found a second pair of spectacles; she cleaned the glasses carefully, stopping from time to time to glance at the boy's face.

"I was niver no fathomer o' handwriting," she said.

He knelt down in front of her, and took her hands in his trembling ones.

"Love me a little first," he pleaded.

Parting the hair on his forehead, she stooped and kissed him. "You're a terrible chile for liking to be mothered," she answered, smiling. "I reckon you laid fine and easy as a baby."

"I never told you anything about my life

before we met," he said; "and you have been very good in not asking."

"I was niver no friend o' questions," she answered.

He was silent a while, and buried his face in her lap, she rubbing her hand softly through his hair. "I was educated by a gentleman under the impression that I was his grandson," he exclaimed at last, and stopped dead.

"Ah!" she said, "I alles knowed you was a gintleman from the first."

"Why, mother," he answered, lifting up his head and smiling at her, "that is hardly a compliment,—you remember you thought I had just been released from jail."

"I was niver no friend to spoiling at sight," she said.

"Well, as things turned out," Humphrey continued, "instead of being his son's child, I proved to be the child of——" he stopped a second time, sinking his face in her lap. She stroked his hair.

"Best leave the story alone, lad," she said; "there ain't no call for nothing so long-winded."

"Ah, it is simple enough," replied Humphrey, simulating ease. "Instead of being the son of the man every one supposed, I turned out to be the son of his servant."

"Ah!" exclaimed the woman, "that's life all over."

"I was a coward," Humphrey continued bitterly; "I wouldn't face things out. I realised after a fashion that Atter's story was true, but I wouldn't face it. I had just been blinded."

"How did that come on you, lad?" the woman interposed.

"An accident," said Humphrey, turning away.

"Poor lad, poor lad."

"Well, I wouldn't face things," Humphrey repeated. "I had only one idea, and that was to get away from the man Atter, my father, you understand; then he was arrested for—manslaughter, and I was free. At Bourke the doctors told me that my blindness would be permanent, but I didn't believe them, and went on to Sydney; the doctors there said the same thing, but I couldn't take it in somehow, and I tried the

Melbourne and Adelaide oculists, and their
opinion coincided with the others. A big
boom was on in Broken Hills when I reached
Adelaide; every other man one met had
turned stockbroker, and to get away from
the misery of things I began speculating.
Just then my grandfather—you understand
whom I mean—wired me out some money—
five thousand pounds. Of course he was still
under the impression that I was his grandson.
I hadn't told him; I hadn't faced things out.
I knew I hadn't any right to the money, but
I took it. I felt a Thursby somehow; it
sounds foolish to say so, but I felt a Thursby;
I felt a Thursby every bit of me. Well—I
speculated with the money and—lost it."

He stopped abruptly and sank his face in
the woman's lap.

"Poor lad," she said, stroking his hair,
"poor lad."

"It's a shabby story, eh, mother?" he exclaimed drearily.

"Poor lad," repeated the old woman, "poor
lad, and you such a gintleman in spite of it;
but there, the Almighty knows who can stand
a dressing and who can't."

"I wrote to my grandfather, I mean—you understand—and owned up, and these letters are in answer to mine."

"They'll be comfortsome, no doubt," said the woman.

"If only I had acted straight, had faced it from the first,—if only I hadn't taken the money——"

But it was contrary to the woman's nature to see faults in those she loved when the hand of fate was heavy upon them.

"I was niver no friend to over remorse," she said, "and now 'twud be as well to read them letters."

There was silence in the small kitchen while the woman held each letter in turn up to the lamp, and laboriously re-read the address.

"I'll take 'em according to date," she remarked at last, opening carefully one of the envelopes, and as carefully extracting the enclosed letter. "Bless us!" she exclaimed, as she smoothed the first page out on the table, "but 'tis fine and controlled, not more than three lines from the first word to the last. I might have written it myself."

"Then it's from my grandfather," said Humphrey; "he detests letter-writing."

"'Tis a fine eddicated hand," exclaimed the old woman admiringly—"'twud most take a gintleman himself to read it; but there, the address is printed on top o' the page."

"Oh, don't bother about the address," said Humphrey, consumed with impatience. "How does it begin?"

"'My dear boy,'" she read, and stopped; he leant his head back against her knee and smiled, he could almost hear the Squire speaking.

"Well!" he exclaimed, and she recommenced.

"'Did I not always tell you you were a young fool?'" she read slowly, and stopped again.

"Ah!" she interpolated, "a gintleman will have his jokes."

"Go on," commanded the boy, and she read the letter steadily on to the end.

"'Come home at once, and give me the pleasure of telling you so in person. En-

8

closed find a draft for a hundred pounds.—
Yours affectionately, JOHN THURSBY.'"

"There," exclaimed the woman, with genuine admiration, "there ain't no mistaking a gintleman when you meet him." But Humphrey was fighting with a lump in his throat, and made no answer. She folded the letter and draft carefully together, and laid them on the little table. "Just as I've said many a time," she continued, running her fingers through the boy's hair with a slow mechanical movement, "the fewer the words, the fuller the sense; that's what comes o' bein' eddicated. Eddication, mark me, is the shortest way there; not that I hold wi' things as they are nowadays, when every frog busts hisself out trying to be took for a bull: there's more in eddication than book-larning, whativer the State may say to the contrary. But there, I ain't no speshil friend to the State,—as I've said to Joe many a time, the State is taking a deal more on itself than becomes it; 'twas all very well in the old days, when it was content wi' the making o' roads and suchlike, but when it takes into its head

that the pudding in my pot is the same size
as my neighbour's, I thank it to let well
alone. It wasn't long after Joe was took ill
that I heard that radical jumbuck William
Harness a-telling him, 'Us ain't got no
masters now,' says he, 'the State is master
now.' 'An' a poor exchange,' I sed; 'if I
am to have a master, let him be o' flesh and
blood the same as meself.' 'Women ain't
got no right understanding in such matters,'
ses he. 'No, nor men either, if the laws be
a token,' ses I; 'why, if I had my will, I'd
disinfranchify the whole lot o' ye!' 'You're
jealous 'cos you ain't got no vote yirself,
Missus,' ses he. 'Women have their dues
the same as the rest,' sed I, 'tho' maybe
their first right should be to stand aside
and hold their tongue.' 'I'm with 'ee there,
Missus,' ses he. Well, well," she added,
folding up her spectacles, and putting them
in the work-basket, "if ther wasn't no laws,
ther 'ud be a sight more unemployed : wot
wi' the making o' 'em and setting o' 'em in
acting they gives a deal o' amusement to the
men; and, bless 'ee, a man likes his bit o'
play the same as a chile. Many's the time

I've said to Joe, 'Take a man to pieces and you'll find he's a chile at heart.'" Humphrey smiled, and gained possession of one of her hands.

"When will you be thinking of going back along home?" she asked.

His face contracted. "There are lots of reasons why I can't go, mother," he said. "Don't you see I've failed in everything."

"You're wonderful frivolous at times, lad," she answered. "And as to failing, ther's two kinds of failing, I reckon: the failing to do what us have marked out for ourselves, and the failing to do what the Almighty has laid down for us; many's the time in missing the first us follers the last, unconscious."

"I like my own programme best, notwith-standing," replied Humphrey.

"Ah, may be," she answered. "I ain't niver yet found the pusson who took to life as 'tis."

"Mother," he said, after a long silence, "if I went home, would you come with me?"

"Faith, no, lad," she answered, "I've given up wearying for the Old Country; after all, it ain't the place but the people that makes home."

"But you haven't many friends here, have you?" he asked gently.

"I wasn't a-talking o' the push,[1] lad; 'twas Joe I was reckoning on."

"You would be so lonely if I left you, even for a time."

The woman looked down on his upturned face, her dim eyes dimmer with tears.

"I won't deny it's pleasant for me to see you about," she said, "but I shan't miss 'ee the same as you think. I niver wanted no other company than Joe's since the first day he comed courting, and us 'ull kind o' pine one for t'other till the same sod covers us both."

Humphrey put his arms round her. "I couldn't leave you, mother, I love you so," he exclaimed.

"Nay, nay, lad," she answered indignantly, "there's the right and the wrong o' things, and you've bin hungering after your own folk this long while."

He did not answer.

She stooped and retied his neckerchief. "I'd liefer that you went," she said.

[1] The crowd, outsiders.

" Mother ? "

" Ay, true ; you're a troublesome chile, and need a deal o' washing and mending. Why, 'twas only this morning that you put on a clean shirt, and as sure as fate you'll be hunting for another to-morrow."

" I've been a terrible trouble to you."

" You ain't spared me, and I'm getting up along in years."

" Mother, mother, what a thoughtless brute I've been ! "

" Well, go right along home then ; outsiders will do your washing," her face contracting as she spoke. "I much misdoubt, though," she added, " if they'll have the same feel for starch."

He put up his hands and felt her face. " Mother," he said, " you're crying ! "

" None such thing," she replied indignantly.

" If I go home, I shall come back again to you—I shall, I swear it."

" Now jest you leave swearing alone ; I ain't no friend to rash promises."

" I don't believe you care for me after all," he said, in a hurt voice.

"You are terrible much a chile, lad," she answered, bending and kissing him.

"If I leave you, tell me something better than 'life's life,'" he said, drawing her face close to his own.

"Ah, lad," she answered, "when a thing *is*, what does us gain by saying it isn't?"

"But it's a dreary philosophy," he pro-tested.

"What do the ills of life matter if us faces 'em courageous?" she answered; but her old, tired voice trembled, for of life and life's ills she was somewhat weary.

Again he drew her face down towards his own.

"Mother," he asked, "did you say life's life when first you knew Joe loved you?"

"Ay, on my knees I said it."

"God bless you for having lived!" cried the boy.

"Oh, lad, lad," she answered, "I was never for denying the Almighty was the Almighty."

THE FAILURE OF FLIPPERTY

THE FAILURE OF FLIPPERTY

PART I

THE great Australian liner steamed west, and Port Melbourne lay a bluer streak on a blue horizon. Passengers were grouped about the deck; and at the stern of the vessel, hidden from the others by a cabin, stood two children, boys. It was evident that they now met for the first time: they looked at one another with shy hesitant interest; both wanted to be friends; each wished the other to make the first advance. In appearance they were strangely unlike: the one was short, broad, with red hair and ears agape; the other, who looked about eleven, was slim, his face small and finely drawn, with a straight, determined little nose, the brow and eyes giving an impression of width and imagination.

The red-headed boy edged nearer. " My

name is Buster," he said, with affected indifference ; "what's yours ? "

"Flipperty," the other answered, " an' I've
got an anchor and two cricket-bats tattooed
on my left arm ; what have you got ? "

Buster's arm did not happen to be tattooed,
so he changed the conversation. " Compare
muscles," he said.

Flipperty bent a little thin arm back to
his shoulder with a great deal of action.

" Putty," commented Buster ; "feel mine."

" You are hard," his companion admitted.

" Practised in the gym every day ; did you
have a good gym in your school ? "

" I never went to school," Flipperty answered, looking ashamed ; but brightening,
" Philip did : Philip's splendid,—why, he
could throw a cricket-ball farther than any
fellow in the college. I'm good at the long
jump."

" Who's Philip ? "

" My brother ; he is at the Teetulpa gold-
fields ; I'm going to help him to dig for
gold."

" You dig for gold ! " Buster interrupted
with scorn ; "why, you look as if you had

sat on a high chair all your life and fed the poor out of a long spoon."

" Well, I just didn't, so there."

" Now, upon your solemn Dick, did you never in all your life give a thing to the poor?"

"Only once, so there," he answered, defiantly.

" What did you give them?"

" Oh, things."

" What things?"

" Shan't say."

" You're afraid."

" I'm not."

" Well, say."

The blood rushed into Flipperty's face and then receded, leaving it quite white. " It was a flannel petticoat," he answered.

"Cracky, do you wear flannel petticoats?" Buster exclaimed, too astonished for further comment. After a moment he added, "I always thought there was something odd about the look of you; I'll tell my brother, —won't he laugh!"

Flipperty caught Buster by the arm and drew him nearer. "Will you keep a secret if I tell you something?" he whispered.

"Fire away; don't take your tongue for a sugar-plum and swallow it."

"Promise?"

"Solemn Dick."

" Well, then, I'm a girl."

" A girl ! "

" Yes."

"Cracky ! "

" Do you think it very wrong ? "

"What, to be a girl?"

" No; to pretend to be a boy ? "

"The police will nab you as sure as an egg."

"Philip won't let them; I'm not afraid."

" They will dress you in yellow and black like a wasp, and paint you all over arrows—solemn Dick. I've seen pictures of thieves in a book."

" I'm not a thief," indignantly.

" What are you, then ? "

" I'm just a girl, who hates being a girl because girls are stupid cooped-up things; so I ran away from home, and now I'm a boy, and I will never be a girl again; so there."

"You a boy ! why, you haven't any more muscle than a cat."

Flipperty appeared not to hear this comment.

"Philip," she said, "is six feet high; I shall grow like him some day."

"Pooh," Buster answered, contemptuously, "you'll never reach four feet on tiptoe; you're small all over,—I daresay you're deformed."

Flipperty changed the conversation. "Philip," she said, "can bowl first-rate yorkers."

"Does he know you're coming?" Buster asked.

"Yes; I wrote and told him."

"Supposing he doesn't get the letter?"

A curious scared expression crossed Flipperty's face. "He will get the letter," she answered, brusquely.

"Supposing he doesn't?"

"I shan't suppose anything of the kind, so there."

"Letters like that always go wrong," Buster declared with emphasis.

Flipperty's eyes filled with angry tears. "I hate you," she said, passionately, "you red-headed, mean-minded, supposing thing."

Her vehemence seemed to surprise Buster. He looked at her a moment in silence, then he took a large red apple from his pocket. "You may have two bites," he said, "as large as you can make them."

A big tear splashed down over Flipperty's face on to the deck. She covered the spot with her foot impatiently.

"The apple is very red," Buster remarked. "Bite just there," he added, indicating the desired spot with a short dirty finger.

Flipperty took a small sobby bite.

"You may eat half," Buster said, "if you promise solemn Dick not to go over your side of the core. Come into my cabin and I'll show you things," he continued, after a pause.

"There," he said, a few minutes later, taking an old pistol from his trunk, "what do you think of that?—it's real. I expect it has killed heaps of people; blew their brains out on the floor—burglars, you know."

"Will it fire off?" she asked.

"No," he replied sadly, "it's broken; but you can pull the trigger. I tell you what," he added, drawing in his breath, "supposing I lend it to you—only supposing, you know."

"Buster, how good you are! but I don't think I shall need it."

His face brightened; he continued to press the pistol on her.

"You will be glad of it," he said, "even if it doesn't go off—sleeping at night with a nugget under your head and murder all around. Why, Flipperty, I daresay you will have to kill a man yourself."

"No," she answered with decision; "I shall let him off. But come and look at the sea, and think of sharks."

"Yes," said Buster. "I wish some one would tumble in, don't you? only a baby, you know, or the boatswain—the cross one with the swivel eye."

"We'd save them," cried Flipperty, flushing; "and nearly get drowned ourselves, and the boatswain would entreat us to ask questions ever afterwards."

"Yes," chimed Buster; "and the captain would let us steer the ship, and beg us to eat more at dessert."

Then they both relapsed into silence, and watched the foam flung back by the churning of the gigantic screw.

9

"Flipperty," said Buster, breaking the silence, "you mustn't cry when we say good-bye to-morrow, or kiss or anything."

She did not answer.

"Promise, solemn Dick," he said.

"I never, never cry, so there," she answered, with an impatient little stamp of her foot; "and, Buster, if you will tell me something very manly, I'll say it."

"Well," he replied, after a pause, "you'd better say 'So-la.'"

"So-la?"

"Yes."

"It sounds rather empty," she objected.

"That's being a man," he answered.

But Flipperty did not look comforted. "It will be very nice seeing Philip to-morrow," she said. "No one in the whole, whole world is as good as Philip."

"If he doesn't come will you go to Tee-tulpa to find him?" Buster asked.

"Yes," she answered.

"You'll lose yourself, as sure as an egg."

"No," she said with decision; "I shall ask questions."

" Supposing your people find you and drag you home ? "

" I've only a stepfather, and he thinks I'm with a horrid smooth-haired girl, who likes sewing and two-and-two walks at school."

" It will cost heaps and heaps to get to Teetulpa."

" I know," she answered. " I've saved all my pennies ever since Philip went away, and my uncle gave me ten pounds on my birthday to buy a pony, and Philip gave me a whole sovereign when he said good-bye."

" I wonder what Philip will say when he sees you ? "

Her eyes filled with tears. " He will say, ' Flipperty, it would have been braver to have stayed at home.' I knew that all along. I tried and tried, because I did want to be brave and grow like Philip, only somehow I never can be brave when he's not there. Philip is quite different from you and me. He doesn't think much of big grand deeds, like the Crusades and that; he says that small, dull, stay-at-home things are harder to do, and ever, ever so much nobler. Why, he even thinks learning to sew noble if you don't like it: of course it isn't noble for the smooth-haired girl."

But Buster was not interested. "Let us steal dessert from the steward," he said.

Early the next morning the steamer anchored opposite Glenelg, and the children watched the approaching tender that was to bring Philip—but he was not on board her.

"Philip hasn't come," Flipperty exclaimed.

"No more he has," echoed Buster; "but perhaps he's found a nugget and is afraid to leave it."

"Yes," she answered sadly; "that must be it."

The tender bell rang, and the passengers who wished to go on shore scrambled down the long companion-ladder.

"You must go now," Buster said.

The tears rushed to her eyes, and she clung to his arm.

"Don't cry," he said. "See," and he produced a large nobby green apple from his pocket; "how much do you bet that I can't get this apple into my mouth at one go?"

She was put into the tender: looking up at the great vessel to say good-bye to Buster,

the "So-la" died on her lips. The boy's
face was a dull purple hue, his mouth wide
open, and tightly wedged inside was the
nobby apple: a compassionate passenger
led him away, and Flipperty saw Buster
no more.

THE Teetulpa express steamed out of the Adelaide station : in the corner of one of the carriages sat Flipperty. The other passengers were men : they took the cushions off the seats, improvised a table, and began playing cards. Gradually the carriage filled with smoke, and Flipperty fell asleep. Every now and again the train would stop at a station, a passenger scramble across her toes, and she would wake and stare drearily out through the smoke-blurred windows. Early the next morning the train reached the terminus : some roughly-built coaches on great leather springs stood outside the station, waiting to take the passengers to the gold-fields. Flipperty climbed on the box of one of the coaches : the other passengers crowded on anywhere—some sat on the roof with their legs dangling over the side. They were a curious mixture of types

—swagmen, shop-boys, gentlemen, larrikins, and the *bonâ-fide* digger. They smoked, swore, spat—spat, swore, smoked.

The coach rolled heavily over the great red sand plain—a plain that stretches its weary length through hundreds of miles of Central Australia. Here and there were patches of blue or salt bush, and a line of bare-breasted gum-trees marked the course of the creek, but of water there was none: the bones of dead bullocks gaped wide against the plain, or an appalling stench and a flock of crows marked the spot where some animal had lately died of thirst and over-work.

A man sitting next to Flipperty eyed her curiously. He was spare, lean, long-legged, and dressed in a flannel shirt and old pair of moleskins, with a short, black, clay pipe stuck in the band of his wide-brimmed hat.

"Only got to pinch his nose for the milk to run out," he said, turning to his companions.

A roar of laughter greeted this sally.

"Was born on the way up," exclaimed a loose-lipped, red-eyed larrikin. "How old may yer be, you blanked little new chum?" he added, turning to Flipperty.

" Eleven," she answered.

" Why, the damned little pup is out on the spree," said the long-legged digger, laughing. " Well, I ran away from home myself when I wasn't much higher than a big-sized cigar : a boy ain't the worse for a bit of spunk. What are you going to do when you reach Teetulpa, little 'un ? "

"Philip and I are going to dig for gold," she replied. " Philip is my brother; he's very big—bigger than you. Buster thinks that Philip has found a nugget already; that's why he didn't meet me. You see he would have to defend the nugget."

There was another roar of laughter, and Flipperty blushed painfully.

" Nuggets ain't so easy found, youngster," the long-legged digger answered. " Fever terrible bad at the diggin's, I hear," he said, turning to his companions. " See a man alive and hearty one morning; the next week yer go into his tent, and there he is lying with his face as black as my hat."

" Why black ? " Flipperty asked.

" Flies," he answered, shortly.

At this moment the conductor came round

to collect the fares; the red-eyed larrikin declared that "he hadn't a blanked cent."

But the conductor, who was a muscular young fellow, had his own especial way of treating impecunious passengers.

"Slack a bit, Bill," he called to the driver.

The horses fell into a slower trot; there was a short struggle, a volley of oaths, and the red-eyed larrikin was dropped off the roof of the coach on to the sand, where he lay swearing so fearfully that the wonder was that he held together. After this episode the other passengers paid their fares.

On they jogged over the great plain. Flipperty fell asleep, and the long-legged digger put his arm around her to prevent her from slipping off the seat.

"Poor little pup," he said, looking down on her tired face—"poor damned little pup."

The sun was sinking west when some one called out "Teetulpa!"

Flipperty saw rows and rows of dirty oblong tents, intersected by half-dug claims. A thick yellow mist hung above the diggings; in some places it seemed to sag down till it almost rested on the tents.

The driver drew up at the store.

" Well, boys, what noos? " he cried to a group of men, who gathered round.

" Gold found at Kidd's gully," one of the bystanders answered. " A nine-ounce nugget; but, darn yer eyes, they stick such lies inter yer that it may be devil's bunkum for all I know."

The long-legged digger turned to Flipperty. " Come inter the store," he said; " we'll see if we can't fix that brother of yours."

The store was a roughly constructed wooden shed with a corrugated iron roof; the interior was divided by a canvas partition running half-way to the roof. The room that they now entered was full of men, some playing cards, others leaning up against the walls, smoking and drinking.

" What name does your brother hang out by? " the digger asked.

" Philip," Flipperty answered,—" Philip Deene."

" Have any of you chaps seen a cove called Deene lately? " he inquired, turning to a group of men standing at the bar.

" Wot's the bally beggar like ? " one of them asked.

" He's very tall," Flipperty answered, " with blue eyes and hair all over curls."

" Ain't clapped eyes on the damned doll," he said, with a coarse laugh.

" There's a long-legged chap called Deene down with the fever," one of the card-players exclaimed, looking round.

" Where does he hang out ? " asked the friendly digger, with a quick glance at Flipperty.

" Foller the creek down past they big gums, and his canvas is the last on the left bank."

The long-legged digger turned and went out of the store, followed by Flipperty. She put her small hand into his rough one, and the man's great fingers, scored with purple scars from the barcoo rot, closed over them. They reached the tent indicated, the digger pushed aside the canvas flap, and Flipperty entered. Lying on some tattered blankets, with parched lips, burning skin, and eyes that failed to recognise her, was Philip.

The child rushed forward. " Philip ! Philip ! " she cried, flinging herself down beside him, "it's Flipperty, your little Flipperty. I couldn't wait, Philip, I couldn't wait."

But he did not answer her.

"Philip, Philip," she sobbed, "Philip, Philip."

The sick man pushed her from him and sprang to his feet.

"I shall be too late," he cried; "O God! I shall be too late." Then he fell forward on his face, unconscious.

The long-legged digger raised him gently and laid him back on the rough bed.

"The poor beggar is half dead with fever," he exclaimed. "You stay here, little 'un," he added, turning to Flipperty, "and I'll see if I can't lay hands on the bally doctor. Great God Almighty, how hot it is! I wonder if I can't fix the flap of the tent back somehow."

The sound of revolver shots echoed through the tent.

"There's some of those drunken devils firing away at each other," he said; "a bullet through the heart of a good round dozen of 'em wouldn't do the credit of the camp any harm. Well, keep your pecker up, little 'un. I'll prospect round for the doctor; half the camp is down with the fever, they say. I reckon I shall have the devil's own work to find him."

Then he went out, leaving Flipperty alone with Philip. She lay down beside him, placed her cheek against his cheek, and her small, thin arms clasped his broad shoulders. The sun sank and swept the long shadows into one uniform grey-black mass; then the moon rose, and its soft light stole across the great plain, making the blue bush look quite soft: it fell, too, on the brother and sister. The hours crept by, but the long-legged digger did not return, nor did Philip wake. The grey light of dawn shivered in the east, and Flipperty realised that Philip had grown strangely cold: she drew the blanket close, and pressed her own little form nearer to him. Then day broke, and as the great plain reddened beneath the sun a vast crowd of flies rose from the ground and entered the tent.

Flipperty gave a shriek of agony: myriads had settled on Philip's face.

Long she knelt and fought an ever-losing battle with the insects : then the doctor entered the tent.

" My poor lad," he said, " your brother is dead."

" The flies," she cried, " the flies are eating his face."

The doctor took off his coat and spread it over the dead man's face.

" They cannot touch him now," he said. " Come outside with me, and we will get some gum-tree boughs to put over him."

" No," she said, " I will stay with Philip."

The doctor went out, and returned in a few moments, his arms full of eucalyptus branches: he crossed the dead man's arms upon his breast, and covered him with the gum-tree boughs. Then he turned to Flipperty, and taking a flask out of his pocket, poured some brandy into a cup.

" Drink this," he said.

She drank obediently.

" You must tell me where to find your people," he asked, kindly.

But she stood staring down at Philip, and did not answer him.

"Poor little chap," the doctor exclaimed softly, turning away. "You must come with me now, like a brave boy," he added.

"No," she answered, "I will stay with Philip."

"My poor little fellow, you can do him no good."

"Go away, go away," she cried, passionately; "I want to be with Philip."

He went out: later in the afternoon he returned, and with him were two men bearing a rough coffin; one of the men was the long-legged digger. There was a look of shame in his face, and he bent down over Flipperty. She was lying with her arms clasped round her brother.

"God strike me for a damned hound," he said, "but I got drunk and forgot yer."

Philip's body was placed in the coffin; it had been made out of old packing-cases— "five prize medals" was painted in big black letters across the side. The lid was nailed down, and they carried the coffin outside the camp to where a rough grave had been dug beneath a great gum-tree. The doctor took a prayer-book out of his pocket, but the burial-service had been torn out.

He began quoting from memory, "'And they shall rest from their labours.'"

"A damned good thing, too," said the long-legged digger.

"Fill up the grave, men, it's too horrible," the doctor exclaimed.

The men fell to work: soon the grave was filled in. Flipperty flung herself down on the spot beneath which Philip lay buried.

"Best leave him alone a bit, lads," the doctor said, in a voice that choked strangely. Then they left her.

Later the long-legged digger returned; with him was another man. Raising Flipperty in his arms, he held her out towards the stranger.

"Her be yer pup, ain't her?" he asked.

"I'm her stepfather."

"Wall," said the long-legged digger, slowly, "her's sleeping now; maybe her'll wake soon enough," and he turned on his heel and left them.

THE BUSTED BLUE DOLL

THE BUSTED BLUE DOLL

DEEP in the Australian Alps is the little town of Omeo. The hills around are scored with worked-out and long-forsaken gold-mines; here and there the thud of the pick may still be heard issuing from some deep shaft; but most of the claims are deserted, and the men who worked them swept away towards other adventures, or lying quiet and ambitionless under the Gippsland sod.

Far up the mountain, where the sarsaparilla hangs from the gum-trees its ragged flame of blue, is a deserted mine; great heaps of yellow mullock line the shaft's mouth; above, the windlass rots out its broken existence; and farther in the shadow an uneven mound, a broad crack, a post with a piece of tin and the name "Battista" scrawled upon it, mark a grave.

One of the early rushes had brought Battista to Australia, and drifted him to the

147

little mining camp among the Gippsland hills.
The men had laughed at his high-pointed hat
with its flapping curves, and at his blue-and-
gold image of the Madonna; but Battista had
wandered under the gum-trees, and paid scant
heed to them. Sometimes he had stooped to
pick up a piece of quartz and rub it absently
on his sleeve; and when the evening came he
had taken up his shepherd's pipe and sounded
once more the airs he had played in the far-
off Abruzzi.

At dawn, as Battista stood and watched the
sun flame up in the east, and fall in a broad
yellow stream upon the Madonna's image, the
thought came to him that there where the ray
fell he would dig for gold, and the idea comforted him: it seemed as if the Blessed Virgin
herself had deigned to point out a way of
escape from this strange and homeless land.
Many days he worked: the yellow mullock-
heaps rose higher beside the rapidly deepen-
ing shaft, when a long-limbed, brown-faced
American "jumped" his claim. Battista had
neglected to procure a licence.

At first he could not understand what had
happened: afterwards, when he realised, he

took his broad keen-edged knife, and laying it at the Madonna's feet, begged her to bless it, and having crossed himself, turned away and went down the mountain-side till he reached the camp. He touched the American on the arm and pointed to his knife; the man from the States laughed lightly; then they drew aside and fought together, and Battista's foot slipped so that his enemy escaped him; but that evening the American sold the mine to Termater Bill the storekeeper for three long drinks and a new swag, going away to try his luck elsewhere. As for Battista, he returned once more to his claim at the foot of the ragged-breasted gum-trees, and here it was that Termater Bill found him.

"I've jest cum," he said, sitting down on a great heap of mullock, "to talk over that blanky claim. I reckon myself there is gold in it."

But Battista answered that, gold or no gold, the mine was his, and he would kill any one who tried to take it from him.

Termater Bill was silent for a while, and spat meditatively down the narrow shaft. At last he observed in an undertone—

" The boys says that jumpt-up busted blue doll o' yers brings luck."

Battista did not understand the allusion to the Madonna, and made no reply.

Again there was a long silence: at last Termater Bill rose and stretched himself. "'Spose," he exclaimed, " I was ter give yer a fifteen years' lease, wi' a half share in the profits, twud be a blanky sight better than a poke in the eye with a burnt stick." But Battista went on digging, and paid no heed to him, till after a while the storekeeper went away.

Time passed by : the great mullock-heaps grew higher, but Battista did not find gold. Sometimes Termater Bill strolled up and asked him if he had " struck that blanky lead yet ? " Then Battista shook his head, but added that he knew the gold was there,—the Blessed Madonna had said so. Termater Bill spat down the long shaft and exclaimed, "That ther jumpt-up busted blue doll gits me quite."

But when night fell and grotesque things moved in and out among the shadows, and the spirit of desolation crept through the bush, then had come into Battista's heart a great weariness of waiting, and he had flung himself down before the image of the Madonna and wept.

And the little blue-and-gold figure had stared out into the gathering darkness with its blank meaningless smile as vacant and as indifferent as before.

It happened that in one of these moments Termater Bill had come to the hut, and Battista, realising that another person was present, sprang to his feet.

"There's gold in that claim," he cried fiercely.

Termater Bill spat on the ground and said, "Thet's so."

"I tell you there is gold in that claim," Battista re-echoed with rising anger.

And Termater Bill spat on the ground once more and repeated, "Thet's so"; then had turned and gone down the mountain towards the camp. "If it warn't for that busted blue doll," he repeated to himself— "the jumpt-up busted thing."

The next day he came again and sat down on an old hide bucket in front of Battista's hut. "I've bin fixin' things up a bit in my mind," he said; "I reckon last night I was a bit ski-wift. Now 'spose," he continued, taking off his hat and placing it before him on the ground, "that thar 'at is the Brown Snake Mine; wall, us knows their main lead runs purty slick to the nor'-east; say yer put in a drive by that tarnation bit o' grass bush," and he spat neatly into the centre of the spot indicated, "wot's ter prevent yer dropping on gold?"

Battista's lips relaxed into a smile. Termater Bill rubbed the sleeve of his shirt across his rough red face, glancing as he did so at his companion.

"Luck is a thundering quare consarn," he exclaimed, after a pause; "I niver bottomed it myself: if yer don't git it, it gits yer, an' I reckon the darned thing is the smartest wi' the gloves."

He took his pipe out of his mouth and pressed his horny thumb down on the red-hot ashes.

"I wudn't lay too much on that jumpt-up blue doll, if I was yer," he said.

Battista smiled. "You don't understand," he answered.

And Termater Bill spat on the ground. "Eh, thet's so," he said, "thet's so."

There was a pause.

"But," began Termater Bill.

"Well?" said the Italian.

"'Tis the tarnation grin on the thing that gits me," the storekeeper burst out, "jest as if her was kinder larfin' at yer; her ain't no mug that busted doll, I'll lay to that."

Battista frowned. "You don't understand," he reiterated.

Again Termater Bill spat on the ground. "Eh, thet's so," he said, "thet's so."

A few weeks later a big bush-fire swept across the hills, and the storekeeper had enough to do without troubling himself about the mine; but when a sudden change of wind sent the fire raging and tearing through the Fainting Ranges and away in the direction of Mount Hopeless, he retraced his steps over the blackened ground till he reached Battista's hut. It was empty: close by the hide rope dangled from the windlass; the woods were silent except for the crashing of some half-charred tree as it toppled over and fell with a great splutter of cinders and wide swirling clouds of soft grey ashes; and stretched face downwards, near the shaft's mouth, the Italian lay dead. Termater Bill turned the body over.

"Pegged out," he said softly—"the blanky cuss has pegged out." Then he turned to the door of the hut and stopped short. "No," he exclaimed, "I reckon I won't: I reckon I cudn't stummick thet God's cuss o' a grin jest yet."

That afternoon they dug Battista's grave beside his claim,—a crowd of idle diggers and dogs looked on. One man, an old fossicker, who was recovering from an attack of the jim-jams (delirium tremens), and whose ideas were still rather hazy, expressed a desire to fight the corpse.

"Git up," he said, "an' I will wrastle wi' yer; git up, yer blanked-out son o' a working bullock, an' I will fight yer for a note."

But the dead man lay still and paid no heed to him.

Termater Bill said he reckoned the company wud 'low him to say a few words.

The company 'lowed him.

Some of the men sat down on the mullock-heaps and began to fill their pipes; others stood about; and one, a jackeroo,[1] took off his hat and then rather sheepishly put it on again.

Termater Bill cleared his throat and spat into the open grave. "Life," he said, "was a jumpt-up quare thing : there wa' they who bottomed payable dirt[2] fust go off, an' thar wa' they who—didn't." He was silent for a moment, and rubbed his face with his sleeve. "But," he continued, "maybe out thar," and he pointed vaguely towards a patch of sunset sky, "across the Divide, they finds colour." [3] He ceased speaking, and the men puffed away at their pipes in silence : at last some one suggested that it was time for the corpse to "turn in."

They lowered the dead man into the grave, —there was no coffin. His arms had stiffened spread-eagle fashion, and he lay sideways against the walls of the grave and looked as if he were about to turn a wheel into eternity. They shovelled back the earth rather gingerly,

[1] Lately arrived colonist.

[2] *Bottom payable dirt*=find sufficient gold to pay working expenses.

[3] *Find colour*=find gold.

avoiding the dead man's face; but, after all, it had to be covered the same as the rest. When they had finished their task they strolled off towards the camp, only Termater Bill remaining behind. He went to Battista's hut and peered through the half-shut door: there in the corner the little blue-and-gold image stared, smiling down inscrutable, indifferent. Long the man gazed back on it; then with sudden determination he entered the hut, and taking Battista's coat from a bench, covered the small figure, then lifting it in his arms, carried it out and flung it down the deep shaft.

But under the gum-trees Battista lay still, silent, satisfied. The years went on, the bottom of the shaft filled with water, and the mullock slipped back into it with a heavy splash; the windlass rotted and grew green, and some one stole the bucket and hide rope; far, far below in the valley the sweet-scented wattle burst into tufted yellow balls, and the blue mists lay on Omeo.

THE ENGLISH GIRL'S CHRISTMAS PRESENTS

THE ENGLISH GIRL'S CHRISTMAS
PRESENTS

SHE had no particular reason for coming to
Dresden, unless it was that a friend had
once told her of two very old, very poor German ladies who kept a pension there, and who
were on bad terms with their pension because
it refused to keep them. The clock in the
Kreutz Kirche struck one as the *droschke*
drew up in front of their door; but the table
in the dining-room was not laid for lunch—
she had come either too early or too late for
the meal. She took two rooms; there were
no other boarders.

It was Christmas week: snow lay on the
ground and Christmas day at the door; there
was a general air of bustle and excitement
about the streets. The pension, however,
remained quiet enough, the two Fräuleins
had not yet begun their Christmas prepara-
tions. The rooms were cold, damp, musty,

—Fräulein Käthe said that "when the fire
was lit, *then!* Hein!" she concluded, holding up her hands, "we have this morning
run out of coals."

The English girl asked them to change a
hundred-mark note, to take the first week's
rent out of it—she needed small money.
Soon a fire was spluttering in the tall china
stove; the two Fräuleins buzzed about it
like bees: they had a half-scared, half-awed
look,—they might almost have been fire-wor-
shippers.

A little later, Fräulein Marta, the younger
of the two sisters, went out to make some
purchases; the English girl went with her.
The Alt Markt, Neu Markt, and each spare
Platz were massed with green fir-trees, all
shapes, sizes, and price. Fräulein Marta's
eyes glowed. "Every German," she said,
"rich or poor, has his tree at Christmas.
We——" she stopped short. "We——"
she stopped again—"ah, possibly this year
we shall have one at our friend's." Depression seemed to fall on her, but it was only
momentary. "Just look at those *Stollen*,"
she exclaimed, flattening her small, round

nose against a confectioner's window. "*Stollen* is our Christmas cake—*Marzipan! Chocolade!* Du lieber Himmel! but there is no time like Christmas. It heals the heart through the eyes."

She stood a moment in front of a stall and fingered some brilliant coloured stuffs lovingly with her worn hands. "My sister," she said, "would call such colours vulgar, but I love the bright things. You," she continued, turning to the girl, "you will have lots of Christmas presents, no doubt. Ach, what it is to be young! We—we shall have many gifts, too: Christmas is for the old and young alike."

The English girl expected no presents, but she did not say so: she felt a little ashamed of her friendless condition, and as the days went on the feeling increased. She gathered from the conversation of the two sisters that they, on their part, were assured of being almost overburdened with gifts.

But then, as they said, "Christmas is Christmas, and one takes the little things and one gives them in the same spirit."

The girl lay awake at night and counted the people who might possibly send her a

present; she could only think of two, and the
more she thought about the matter, the
more certain she became that this year they
would neglect to do so. The moment came
when she would have telegraphed to them,
" For Heaven's sake send me a present "—
but Christmas Eve had already arrived.

Reduced to despair, she determined at last
to buy herself a number of presents, and tell
the sisters that they had been given to her by
friends. She bought things that she needed,
—pins, sealing-wax, string : then the thought
struck her that, should either Fräulein Käthe
or Marta ask to see the contents of such parcels, they would certainly fail of being im-
pressed. So she went out a second time and
tried to look at the shops with their eyes, and
buy things that they would think beautiful.
On her return she hid her purchases deep
down in her trunk. She was still on her knees
before the box when Fräulein Marta entered.
The girl blushed, shame-faced; the Fräulein
seemed also a little discomposed.

" You will be dining to-morrow with friends,
no doubt," she said. " We also shall—dine
with—friends."

The English girl knew no one in Dresden. "Oh—ah yes, of course," she said, "I shall be dining with friends—several friends."

Fräulein Marta smiled down upon her: "*Fröhliche Weihnacht*,—Merry Christmas, as you say in your country."

"Merry Christmas," the girl repeated, with a sob in her throat. "Dear old Christmas, I love it—don't you?"

"Yes," answered the old woman, simply; "I have always loved it,—even—when—well, well——" she stopped. "See," she added, with a half shiver, "how thickly it snows."

"Sit by the fire and tell me things," said the girl.

Fräulein Marta's face brightened: "My sister knows so many more stories than I do. Shall I call her?"

"Will you?"

But when the two sisters sat before the high white china stove the heat seemed to make them drowsy, and they fell asleep.

Christmas day brought the girl a number of letters and parcels which she had posted over-night. She laid them in a conspicuous place on the table, but the two Fräuleins seemed occupied with their own affairs, and did not glance that way. The evening came; the candles on the Christmas trees were lit, and round them children big and little crowded with eyes and mouths wide open, expectant. The English girl went out into the streets, crossed the Bürgerwiese, and entered the Grosser Garten. It had been freezing hard,—the ground clanged like metal beneath her feet; from time to time a branch split off short from beneath its weight of snow, and the air below the ice-bound ponds growled heavily. Leaving the road for a narrow foot-track, she pierced deeper into the solitude. A great self-pity fell upon her,—she sobbed because every one in the whole world was more happy than she : even the two Fräuleins had friends; they were not obliged to buy presents for themselves,—and she sobbed again. High up in the sky the moon kicked a way through the heavy clouds, but the stars were hidden. Suddenly the girl heard voices; unnoticed by herself she had approached a summer-house. She drew nearer, and, peering in, saw the two sisters.

Far away in the town the Kreutz Kirche clock tolled nine.

Fräulein Marta sighed. " Are you cold, sister ? " she said. " In another half hour we might go home."

" Ah yes, in another half hour; but what shall we do if she asks to see the presents ? "

" Perhaps she may not ask; I was careful not even to glance at hers." The girl stole away, and, hurrying back to the house, lifted the presents out from the trunks and wrote on them Fräulein Marta and Käthe's names, then, making them into one big package, went out again into the night. The snow fell softly upon her as she stood in the street waiting for the two sisters to return home. At last she saw them cross the Platz, their thin figures bent, as if they were afraid of the white light that the snow flung back upon them. They cast a fugitive look round, before entering their house. The door clanged close on their heels, the echo ringing down the street. For a moment the girl stood and listened to it, then moving away, she found a dienstman, gave him the parcel containing the presents, and told him to deliver it at the pension. When she returned later, Fräulein Marta called her into the dining-room. "Sehen Sie nur," she said, pointing at the presents that lay unpacked upon the table; "Christmas is Christmas for old and young alike."

THE RED-HAIRED MAN'S DREAM

THE RED-HAIRED MAN'S DREAM

CHAPTER I

DUSK had fallen on the close of a March afternoon, when, the train having bumped slowly across the Roman Campagna, stopped at Valmonte station and deposited two English girls. A few minutes later it crawled away, and the two girls scrambled up on the yellow diligence, with its big, flapping leather hood. The driver mounted the box, the three horses broke into a gallop, the long-lashed whip cracking loud and clear in the gathering darkness. A man, seated face to his donkey's tail while the animal drank, gazed mildly after them.

The younger girl glanced at him a moment, then, laying her hand on her friend's knee, "How unlike all this is to England, Jess!" she said. The other was silent a moment, staring out into the gathering darkness.

"I was born in a queer old grey stone house on the border of Exmoor," she exclaimed at length. "I learnt to love those moors, with their look as if the peace of God had settled on them and couldn't be rubbed off."

"It is a long time now since you were in England," her friend said, reflectively. "Don't you ever want to see your old home again ? "

"Home ! " Jess repeated in a bitter voice. "I have no home; it was sold years ago when my parents died. Ah, Roch, I hate the past ! Don't let us talk about it; " and they both relapsed again into silence.

The clock had struck eleven when they reached Olevano : the village stared down indifferently at them, looking as if it needed all its strength to cling to the rocky ridge on which it had obtained foothold. The old castle, the tall, narrow clock-tower, and the lichened roofs, lay wrapt in shadow. Around, the Hernican Mountains guarded the silence, and in the valley the mist, like some huge serpent, slept heavily. A few minutes later the girls were climbing up the crumbling

steps that led through the village to the
Albergo. Every now and again the rays
from the lamps, mixing with the moon-
beams, would light up the entrance of some
grim stone house, where below, in an atmos·
phere thick with smells, the inhabitants—
pigs included—slumbered. A gate admitted
them to an olive-garden, at the end of which
rose an irregular, battered house,—it was the
Albergo.

Roch gave a sigh of relief as she clam-
bered up the steps and opened the creaky
door.

Standing close to the lamp was a tall, gaunt
young Englishman: his head was bent, and
sagging down on his forehead was a tumbled
mop of red hair. In his hands, which were
grotesquely big, was a kitten, and from one
of its paws he was extracting a thorn. For
a moment they regarded each other in silence ;
then, the thorn extracted, he placed the kitten
upon the ground, and Jess entering at the
same time, he noticed that she was lame, and
that she looked tired and sad : the expression
of annoyed surprise which had gathered on
his face passed away.

"I will hunt up the padrona," he said. "I am afraid every one has gone to bed."

"Did you see his hands ! " Roch exclaimed, when she and her friend were left alone to-gether.

" Whose ? " Jess asked, inattentively.

" Why, the Red-haired Man's," Roch answered.

CHAPTER II

Roch rose early next morning, pulled back the worm-eaten green shutters, gave one glance at Olevano, where it lay sunning its old, patched walls, and then concentrated her attention on dressing. Later, when she entered the village, she was greeted by the grunting and snorting of innumerable pigs. Roch, fresh and charming herself and in no wise dismayed, nodded to the women with the water-cans and baskets of hot polenta on their heads, and they, in their turn, smiled back at her. At the foot of the hill a boy was playing ruzzola: passing him, she followed a small path that branched off from the main road, leading upwards. Before her and around lay the bracken-covered hills, here and there a group of olive trees; a freshly turned patch of earth marked where some peasant had scrawled his laborious pot-hooks. As Roch strolled along she saw above her, lying full length on a sloping bank, the Red-haired Man, and seated astride across his chest was a small, bullet-headed child about two years old. The Red-haired Man appeared to be wrapped in profound slumber, hat drawn down over his eyes and big loose-jointed hands clasped behind his head. The baby, on the contrary, was much awake, and Roch began to make faces at it: the child responded with a fat crow of delight, thumping the man's chest to emphasise approval. Roch glanced round: no one being in sight, she picked up her skirts and executed a wild jig; the baby gave one chuckling scream, lost its balance, rolled rapidly down the sloping bank, and lay, a fat little lump of surprised, pleased alarm, at Roch's feet. The Red-haired Man jumped up, blushing violently.

"Dear me," exclaimed Roch, glancing at the baby in apparent astonishment. "Where did it come from?"

"It is Pico, the washerwoman's baby," he answered, stiffly. "I borrowed it."

"And do you roll it up and down banks all day?"

"I was asleep."

"Is that how you take care of babies when you borrow them?"

"It would never have fallen if you hadn't made faces at it."

"I thought you said you were asleep."

The Red-haired Man appeared not to hear the remark.

"Now, tell me," Roch exclaimed with interest, "was it a good work you were doing? Were you trying to improve the poor by showing them beautiful scenery? Because if you were, I assure you it is quite useless."

His wide mouth expanded into a smile, showing a row of strong white teeth.

Roch decided that it was a pleasant smile, but then, it was on so gigantic a scale, there was room for something pleasant to creep in.

"No," he answered, "I was trying to improve myself."

"Oh how?" she asked, genuinely astonished. The colour rushed into his face: the

Red-haired Man had a detestable habit of blushing.

" Babies believe in things," he said, lightly. "They believe in themselves, in you, in the world in general."

Roch was silent a moment, scanning him with some attention. His face, boyish in spite of its gauntness, was that of a man whose first tussle with facts was yet to come, and who was ignorant alike of the powers or passions that were slumbering in him.

" You must be very——" she stopped short.

" What ? " he asked.

" *Young*," she said, slowly.

There was a pause : it is possible that, at moments, the Red-haired Man had himself been haunted by such a thought.

His manner stiffened. " Woman's lack of penetration is proverbial," he answered.

" H'mn," said Roch, turning away, " h'mn." She walked a few paces, halted, and glanced back at him. He was still standing at the top of the bank, gazing indignantly in her direction.

" Can you speak Italian ? " she asked.

" A little," he answered, with cool terse-

ness. He had no desire to prolong the conversation.

"Well," she replied, returning once more
to the foot of the bank. "Will you buy me
a pig?"

"A pig!"

"Yes, it is the fashion in Olevano. Now,
if you had had a *pig* with you this morning
instead of a baby—dear me," glancing round
as she spoke, "where *is* the baby? Why,"
she continued, flinging away her sunshade
and running along the path, "there it is
crawling down a precipice."

With a couple of strides the Red-haired
Man had cleared the bank and was past her;
the next moment he had grabbed Pico, dragging him back into safety by the heels.

"How careless you are," cried Roch, who
had been thoroughly frightened. "Just
think," she added indignantly, "in another
instant it might have been killed."

His face was very white. "I shan't think
anything of the kind," he replied with equal
indignation, "because it is saved."

"Saved!" she exclaimed. "Why, you
are holding it by the heels!"

The Red-haired Man hastily righted Pico, who, astonished at the marvellous yet involuntary evolutions he had been made to perform, was howling with some lustiness.

"Give it to me," said Roch. "You are not fit to be trusted with a child."

"I shall do no such thing," he answered, fiercely.

Roch looked at him, and then burst into a peal of laughter.

"Well," she said, "the sooner that baby gives up believing in you the better." Then she proceeded on her way, leaving the Red-haired Man consumed with indignation.

CHAPTER III

A few days later Jess was sitting under the Albergo loggia when the Red-haired Man joined her. He glanced down as she leant back in the rocking-chair, remembering, with a pang of pity, that she was lame. It seemed to him that this lameness probably accounted for the bitter expression of her face : it was a strange, contradictory face ; well-bred in detail, there was a certain nobility about the

12

wide brow and full-couraged eyes, but the
mouth, thin, hard, compressed, was the mouth
of a middle-aged, disappointed woman. Yet
the girl was young enough—twenty-two, at
most. Looking at her, he found himself
wondering whether the lips would grow full
and soft if kissed: they were not the lips a
man would feel much inclination to kiss—she
was in so great need of love, the chances were
she would never get it. He felt a great pity
for her: a woman, he told himself, is not a
woman unless she is loved—she remains a
half-finished sketch of something she might
be. Then Jess looked across at him and
smiled,—her smile raised the veil between
herself and him; for a brief moment he saw
sheer down into her heart, and all that he saw
was beautiful. He had a sudden sense of
nearness, a belief that he had known this
woman elsewhere.

"I suppose it is improbable," he said, "but
I have a strange feeling that we have met
before."

"Most improbable," she answered; "I
have not been in England since I was a
child."

"But it is long ago that I seem to remember you."

"Ah!" she exclaimed slowly, as some vague recollection began to take shape in her mind.

"Do you know Devonshire?" he asked, with sudden quick glimmer of facts.

"Yes, but we lived in an out-of-the-way part. Gorston was the nearest place, and it was hardly within driving distance."

"It was there I must have met you. Old Froude Gorston is my uncle!" he exclaimed.

Then she remembered, and put out her hand with an instinctive movement as if to push the subject from her; but he, unconscious of her distaste, continued: "I used to spend my holidays at Gorston. Very good trout-fishing in some of those streams, at least I thought so in my boyish days. Why, it was trout-fishing, and you must have been—but you weren't lame." He stopped, and his face suddenly blanched. "Great Heavens!" he exclaimed; "it wasn't that jump, the jump from the rock that I made you take, that caused your lameness?"

"Of course not," she answered, hastily.

"You had nothing to do with it." A sudden conviction came to him that she was not speaking the truth.

"How did it happen?" he asked, in a harsh voice.

"Why talk about it?" she replied, gently. "Tell me about yourself. How strange that you should have recognised me after all these years!"

"Then I am responsible," he said. It was horrible to him to be the indirect cause of suffering to any one.

"No, no," she answered. "I should have jumped whether you had been there or not: the rock always had a fascination for me. Besides," she continued, trying to turn his attention from the subject, "it was the little book that I wanted. I remember in those days I had a ridiculous belief that in some book lay the secret of how to escape from unhappiness —though I am afraid that, as far as I am concerned, the secret has remained unanswered."

He was full of bitter self-accusation. "I went back to school the next day and thought it was only a sprain. How could I have been such a fool!" he said.

"Why should you have thought other-wise?" she replied. "Do you remember how good you were to me? You carried me almost all the way home. You were strong even in those days,"—she smiled at the involuntary recollection of him that rose before her, a lanky, grotesque, red-haired boy, but infi-nitely, awkwardly gentle.

"And I have spoilt your life," he said.

"Do you never learn to judge things with reasonable common-sense?" she answered, with a touch of impatience. "Besides, lame-ness is not the same trial to a woman as it is to a man."

"But still it is lameness," he inter-rupted.

She rose from her chair, and drew closer to him. "Do you think it has not also had its good side?" she said. "Do you think it has not been the cause of a hundred little acts of kindness which, otherwise, I should have gone without? People are not ungenerous; but they are in a hurry. Well, this lameness, which you think so terrible, has made them stop and ask themselves if they could do something for me. I have noticed it over

and over again; my childhood was solitary
enough—I do not suppose that any one cared
for me unless it was Nanny, my old nurse;
but I know she never loved me before my
accident as she did afterwards. Don't you
think," and she stopped a moment and smiled
at him,—"don't you think," she continued,
"that a little love is worth a lot of lameness?
because if you don't, I do."   She put out her
hand; he grasped it in his big, strong fingers,
and the boyish tears came into his eyes. She
saw them, but pretended not to notice, talking on to avoid silence.

"Poor Nanny," she said; "I don't think
she ever got over my being sent to school in
Germany. 'A 'eathen land,' she called it, 'a
'eathen land.' I believe she thought it was
inhabited by blacks. She always wrote on
my birthday and sent me a card. Her letters
were rather hard to read, because each word
began with a capital, and she had a confused
notion as to the difference between y's, l's, and
g's, but they were the only letters I ever received. I don't think I cared very much
whether I could read them or not. The card
too was always the same; it represented a

long pinkish hand holding a cabbage-shaped purple rose. Somehow, the fact that it was always the same comforted me. I knew, too, where she had bought it, and I used to lie awake at night and picture her going into the small shop at the end of the village. It was kept by an old woman named Rogers, who had never had any teeth. She sold a thin, flat sort of gingerbread that the poor people called 'fairin,' and if you spent more than fourpence, she would open her mouth and tap her gums with a long wooden spoon that she used to ladle out her brown sugar. ''Ard ez horn,' she would say, ''ard ez horn.' Nanny is dead now: I don't know that I ever did much to make her life happy; but the only moments in my childhood I care to look back on I owe to her."

She was silent a moment, and the bitterness left her face.

"Don't worry over that stupid episode," she said. "We were both children, and I am a strong believer in Fate."

"Fate," he repeated; "that is a paralysing belief—have nothing to do with it."

"Each forms his theory on his own experience," she answered, "and mine has made me pessimistic."

"We have always the Future," he said. "I am glad that we have met again."

"Ah!" she answered, "I am wiser than you—I always wait to be glad."

His face contracted. "Your theory is all wrong," he said. "Enjoy the minutes; the long hours will take care of themselves."

She saw that he was hurt. "We won't bother about the theory this time," she exclaimed, with quick compunction.

He smiled. "No," he said, "we won't bother about the theory, and we will make a little grab at happiness. Is it a pact?"

"Yes," she replied, returning the smile, "it is a pact."

CHAPTER IV

"The pig has arrived, come and see it," cried Roch a few days later, bursting into Jess's room. "It is very small, and has two crinkles in its tail. But first put on your hat, because the Red-haired Man has found you a mule, and we are all going to pick white heather on the hills. There," she added a moment later, when Jess limped down the steps, "there it is," pointing at a little black object that was struggling violently in a peasant woman's arms.

"I have paid three paoli more for its manners," she continued, in a triumphant voice; "I shall call it Felice. I am sure that it is a very happy little pig."

"The Signorina is fond of bacon," said the peasant woman, sympathetically.

"Oh!" exclaimed Roch.

"What did she say?" Jess asked.

"She talks patois," Roch explained hurriedly; "I couldn't translate it."

"Ah!" the woman continued, "it comes from a well-favoured stock, does that pig. It was only on the day of the blessed St. Joseph that I salted down its own brothers, and if the Signorina pleases, I will bring her a spare rib that she may taste it herself."

"What a horrid woman," exclaimed Roch, growing crimson.

"Please tell her to put the pig down and tie a string round its leg," she continued, turning to the Red-haired Man, who joined them at this moment. "I will go on; I am sure that Felice needs exercise; Jess, you can easily catch me up on the mule."

No sooner did the pig regain terra firma than it clattered grunting and squealing down the path, Roch, in the rear, holding tight to the string, with a breathless energy worthy of a better cause. The woman watched them in astonished despair.

"Madonna mia!" she exclaimed, wringing her hands, "but the Signorina's pig will never grow fat."

Jess and the Red-haired Man followed more slowly with the mule. She glanced down at his big form as he strode beside, and deftly prevented the overhanging boughs from touching her, and was conscious of a curious subtle pleasure in her own weakness. The path led through a small wood; descending precipitous fashion, it turned a sudden angle and wound round the hills, where the wild thorn bushes thrust their shaggy white heads out from among the bracken. Below, in the valley, a yellow-faced stream hustled along, while innumerable rivulets scrambled over the bare grey rocks, leaving a glistening

track as if the stroll of some Brobdingnagian
snail had taken him past that way.

It was very pleasant to the Red-haired Man
to wait upon this woman, to help her in some
small way; his pulses beat with a big boyish
happiness.   He put his hand on the flap of
the saddle : "A man is some use in the world
when he can protect a woman.   Why don't
you need more protection?" he asked, his
mouth expanding into one of its gigantic
smiles.

She was so unused to being protected, her
eyes filled with tears at the thought.   When
he saw the tears and the trembling of her
lips, the strings of his heart vibrated like a
resonant chord.

"Life has it's good things," he said,
"though I don't believe you have tasted
them yet."

She did not answer : she had a great longing for life's good things, but she was also
afraid of them,—she was so certain that happiness had to be paid for with tears.   In the
silence the mule's hoofs pattered sharply on
the rough ground; little black and green
lizards scuttled away through the dried grass,

making a pretence of being more frightened than in truth they were. A sudden bend in the road brought them in sight of Roch, who was hurrying in their direction.

" Come quickly, please," she cried. "There are two artists asleep under a rock. Felice is eating up their sketch-books. I can't get her away, and the fattest artist looks as if he were going to wake."

The Red-haired Man ran off in the direction in which she pointed, and Roch, having placed the responsibility on his shoulders, followed more slowly behind; but, hearing excited voices, she climbed a neighbouring rock from which she could obtain an advantageous yet safe view of the situation.

" Potztausend Donnerwetter ! " cried the fat artist, pointing at an uninviting clumped up heap upon the ground. "You will me say dat is my skedch-book,—dat my lofely drawings ? "

" H'mn humph, 'pon my word, h'mn humph," replied the Red-haired Man. " It looks uncommonly as if it might be."

At this moment the pig, endeavouring to escape, ran over the face of the other artist.

"Du lieber Himmel!" he exclaimed, jumping to his feet. "Was geht vor?"

"Ach! it is a forreign verdamnter Schwein that eats our things," the fat man cried, wringing his hands.

"Was," replied the other, "the picture I did make of the lofely Mädchen. Gott bewahre, es ist nicht wahr. You sir, you Englecsh sgentleman," he continued, in a voice of rising anger, as the full extent of his loss came home to him—"I ask you how came that Schwein here to be?"

"H'mn humph, most unfortunate occurrence," the Red-haired Man said. "Hang it all," he ended, abruptly. "Confound you and the pig together."

"Confound me and the pee-ig," spluttered the German, choking with anger. "I have, you know that in our land we ask for such to the duel."

"Pooh!" said the Red-haired Man. "Pooh!"

"Pooh!" repeated the artist, fiercely, "pooh! It is noding to do with pooh. Ach, Engleeish Meess," he continued, catching sight of Roch, "you laugh? Is it dat I do see you laugh?"

"Oh, no!" exclaimed Roch, hurriedly, "oh, no!"

"To who belongs that Schwein?" interposed the fat German, taking out his notebook. "How calls the man his name?"

"He bought it," cried Roch, pointing at the Red-haired Man. "He's responsible." Then she slithered down the rock, and, running up to Jess, who was approaching on the mule—"Fly, fly," she cried, in breathless excitement; "they want our names."

"Were they very angry?" Jess asked, as the mule ambled down a little side path.

"Very," assented Roch.

"It must have been awkward," pursued Jess. "Did you explain how it happened?"

"Oh! they were Germans."

"I thought you spoke German."

Roch did not answer. "Here comes the Red-haired Man," she exclaimed.

"Well," he burst out, "if all girls behave——"

"How unchivalrous you are, abusing women," Roch interrupted. "Men always complain that women nowadays want to do everything for themselves. I am sure I have never wished to carry my own parcels, and on the very first opportunity a man is rude to me."

"Rude," he repeated, hotly. "I don't want to be rude; but there are limits——"

"Where is Felice? You have not left her behind?" she cried, turning on him.

"Yes," he said, "and those Germans will have made her into a sausage by now."

"Oh, how brutal men are!" Roch exclaimed. "My poor dear little Felice," and she began to run back towards the big rock with quick, wavy steps, that seemed to require a great deal of energy for the small portion of ground over which they progressed. A couple of strides, and the Red-haired Man had caught her up.

"Don't bother, I will get your pig," he said, gruffly.

"I can't trust you," she sobbed, "you're too mean."

"Why, there is the detestable little pig hunting about by itself in the bracken," he exclaimed, with some relief. "Now, do sit down and I will catch it for you."

"Dear Felice," said Roch; "don't pinch her."

"As if I should pinch a pig," he answered
indignantly, striding away. But it was one
thing to promise to catch Felice and quite
another to do it, and Roch, whose tears were
soon dried, burst into peals of laughter, as
she watched the Red-haired Man pursuing
the pig round the thorn bushes and over the
slippery grey boulders. Once, when Felice,
hard pressed, ran close by, her mistress made
no endeavour to catch, but instead cheered
her back into the fray.

At last the Red-haired Man returned with
Felice grunting protestations under his arm.

"Just look at my coat," he exclaimed, indignantly. "Torn to rags!"

"I never could have believed a pig could
run so far and keep so cool," said Roch, in a
surprised voice. "Oh, Jess, there you are!"
she added, as the latter joined them. "Do
let us sit down and enjoy ourselves. What
a pleasant world it is! Whenever I see a
view I am always afraid that some author
will come by and describe it. Dear Felice,"
she continued, glancing in apparent admiration at the little pig, "how pretty you are,
and how happy you look! Happiness is

hereditary in our family—none of us can
escape it.   When my great-great-grandfather
had reached some marvellous age, he said he
would like to live each moment of his life
again.   I believe every one was relieved when
he didn't, because he took snuff.   There was
an old woman in our village who took snuff ;
she lived to be a hundred, grew fresh hair,
new teeth, and died before she could use
them.   They put on her tombstone—

'Her grawed a fresh load o' hair on the tap o' her head,
But before she could comb it, by Gosh her was dead.'

Only the clergyman, 'old Passon Bellew,' as
the villagers called him, insisted on the words
being erased, so they just wrote : ' 'Twas the
teeth that carried her off—"Go thou and do
likewise."' I think that was the text. I often
wonder if it was the snuff that made all that
happen.   I borrowed some from her once and
gave it to the cat during prayers: she flew up
the back of a fat little bishop who was staying
with us.   My brothers and I giggled so loud
we were obliged to turn it into an Amen.
Now Jess, when you look like that, I know
you are concocting ideals, or thinking about

13

right and wrong or other disagreeable things.
I never can understand why people are so
anxious to know what is right when it is so
much more convenient not to. Oh, Felice
has eaten up all the chocolates!" she exclaimed, with an abrupt change of subject.
"I do think that the three paoli paid extra
for her manners were quite thrown away."

In the general commotion that ensued the
sun sank: for a while the mountains glowed
porphyry red, and then drew a veil blue as
lapis-lazuli across their none too modest faces.
The valleys, crammed with shadows, lay
crumpled and forlorn,—the maid in the nur-
sery ballad, who was tossed by a cow, could
not have looked more disconsolate.

Roch bent down and gave Jess a suspicion
of a kiss, just where her brown hair curled
back from the nape of her neck.

"Dear Jess," she exclaimed, lightly, though
there was a sound of tears in her voice, "how
battered you will be when you reach heaven;
but then, I am sure you will get there!"

The Red-haired Man's eyes rested on the
two girls, but it was only Jess that he saw.
"Yes," he told himself, "life so far had been

hard to her, but it should not always be hard."

Roch glanced at him, and something in the expression of his face thrilled her strangely.

CHAPTER V

A NARROW foot-track leads from the Albergo past the cemetery, winding round the hills above Olevano. Opposite, on its great pointed mountain, is Rocca di Cava, washed up there in the middle ages and left stranded, crimes and all, while the centuries strode on, knocking the outside world into other forms, and whispering to it other ideas. Along this path, late one afternoon, Jess limped somewhat wearily, for walking was always a painful exertion to her. At last an old broken stump offered a resting-place, and sitting down, she turned to look at the sun, as it tossed its beams at the clouds, and they, colouring with exertion, cast them in their turn, in great flakes of orange, gold, and umber, on the patient sky. Absorbed in watching, she hardly noticed the Red-haired Man stood beside her, and yet something

that stirred within him, something which
had drawn all the dreaminess out of his
face, troubled her unconsciously.

A stray gleam from the fast-setting sun fell
on him, throwing into relief his muscular
figure and the strength and weakness of his
face. He bent down and laid his hand upon
her arm.

"Do you remember once telling me," he
said, "that love was worth a great deal of
lameness, and I——"

She had risen to her feet. "You," she
interrupted, "you pity me, and I am not
sure," her voice broke, "that I am altogether
grateful."

"Who is talking of pity? I love you," he
exclaimed, trying to draw her towards him.

She shrank back. "It is all so sudden,"
she said, helplessly.

"Does that make you afraid," he asked,
"when you feel, you know, that it is true?"

She loved him, but the intense happiness
that his love would bring made her distrust
its existence.

"I feel nothing except that you are deceived," she answered; then a sudden fierce

despair swept away her self-control. "Oh, I hate pity!" she cried, passionately. "Hate it! hate it!"

"It is you who are deceived," he said. His strong arms closed round her and drew her straight up against his breast. "We love each other, and you are mine," he ended, his voice vibrating with a resistless rush of feeling.

She broke into bitter, tearless sobs. "It is a dream," she said, "a desolate, deceiving dream." And yet she knew that, dream or no dream, it was too strong for her—she could not fight against it. But the Red-haired Man had no fears. He raised her face, which drooped half ashamed against his breast, and kissed her.

"Men do not sleep so soundly, dear one," he answered. "When you have trusted yourself to me,"—a passion of tenderness shook him,—"when you are my wife, you will learn that it is no dream." As he spoke she opened wide her heart to the coming joy or grief, she knew not which awaited her.

"Dearest," he said, "tell me that you are not afraid. Tell me that you are glad."

"I am glad," she whispered.

A wave of exultation swept over him.

"And it is worth the past pain?" he asked, with fierce, impatient joy.

"It is worth the past pain," she repeated, softly.

"And the pain of the future?"

She drew a quick, trembling breath. "That too!" she said.   Later they walked on : the path was uneven,—she leant upon his arm.

"Jess! Jess!" he exclaimed, turning to her, "tell me you are glad that you are lame."

She smiled through her tears.   "I am glad," she answered, "glad, glad."

"See," he said, "see how rough the path is—I must carry you."   He raised her in his strong arms. · At the foot of the hill he put her gently down.

"Dearest," he said, "it is good that we love each other."   But she, trembling, answered nothing.

The sun sank, and the stars shot out, rather reluctantly.   "How strange," said Jess, at last, "that it is me you love and not Roch."

"She is a child," he answered, smiling.

"No, she is not a child," Jess said, "and she is very beautiful."

He stooped and kissed her. "Is she?" he answered, indifferently. "I do not think I have ever noticed it. I believe I have always been looking at you."

CHAPTER VI

OLEVANO cannot boast of many woods, but, strolling along, the Red-haired Man had come on a group of trees gathered round a small brown-faced pool that lapped in their shadows as a starved cat milk. Near it was seated Roch, engaged in a somewhat heated controversy with her little black pig on the subject of education.

"Now, Felice," she exclaimed, "what objection can a loyal, intelligent pig have to die for the Queen?"

Felice refused to state her reasons in words, but, having whisked her small, curly tail, made a frantic endeavour to scuttle away. The effort, however, proved unsuccessful, and her attention was once more drawn to the subject in question.

"Oh, Felice!" the girl remonstrated, "when it is not only dying, but chocolates afterwards!"

At the mention of chocolates the little black pig cocked up one ear, and appeared to reconsider the question.

"When you look like that," cried Roch, flinging her arms round Felice, "you are the very dearest little pig that ever, ever was made. And I tell you what," she added, magnanimously, "we will eat all the chocolates up ourselves, and not bother about the Queen."

In the silence that followed the proposition a chuckle made itself heard, and Roch, glancing round, saw the Red-haired Man trying to dodge behind a tree.

"How mean you are, watching!" she exclaimed, angrily.

The Red-haired Man came nearer, and flung himself down on the grass, Felice utilising the opportunity to scamper off and make private investigations on her own account.

"I never saw a more intelligent pig in my life," he answered, with conviction. Roch was not quite sure how to take this remark, so she changed the subject.

"Now, while I remember it," she said, "what *is* your name?"

"My name?" he repeated in astonishment. "You don't mean to say that you haven't learnt that yet? Why, what do you call me?"

"Oh!" she exclaimed, getting a little red, "that is quite easy. One thinks of characteristics."

"Characteristics? What characteristics?"

"Well, what do you think?" she asked.

"Think," he repeated. "H'm, hum, humph. I'm tall."

"Yes," she answered, in a voice that somehow had the effect of diminishing his height. "You're tall."

"And strong," he said, surveying himself with justifiable pride.

"So are most men," she remarked, sniffily.

"And heavy," he said, interrupting her.

"*What* a thing to boast of!" she exclaimed, in genuine surprise.

"Bother characteristics," he said. "I can't think of anything else."

"Can't you *really* guess?"—in an astonished voice.

"No," he said.

"Why, what *do* you think made the bull run at you the other day?"

"The bull run at me?"

"Why, what colour is your hair?" she said in desperation.

"The same colour as yours, of course."

She was almost too astonished for speech. "Oh," she cried at last, "mine's auburn!"

"Pouf!" he said; "I see no difference."

"Come, and look for yourself," she exclaimed, excitedly, pulling him towards the little brown-faced pool.

They both knelt down in front of it: there was a moment's silence.

"Well," cried Roch, "what do you see?"

He saw a small, oval face; eyes deeply blue, peering down, full of anxiety, at the reflection of the chestnut hair that curled out, glinting with gold, and scrambled along the edge of her broad white forehead. The short nose, tip-tilted, delicate, expressed a faint, questioning surprise; the mouth too large to be small, freshly, childishly red, curved back indignant, only the dimple that had been pressed into the chin was content in its own happiness, and refused at all costs to express anything but pleasure. His eyes rested on her face, lingeringly, then they followed the lines of her white throat till they rested on the soft curves that proclaimed her woman.

" Well ? " cried Roch again, " well ? "

No answer.

"Oh, *don't* you see the difference ? " she exclaimed, almost in tears.

The Red-haired Man raised himself, breathing heavily.

" What colour is it ? " she cried, wringing her hands with impatience.

He looked at her in a dazed, dull way, as if he were blind as well as dumb.

" Do speak ! " she cried, catching him by the coat. " You must—you must see the difference."

" The difference," he repeated, in a far-away voice. " What difference ? "

" Oh, how stupid you are ! " she exclaimed, despairingly. " Is my hair red ? "

He drew a deep breath, pulling himself together. " Red ! " he cried. " It flames, it

glows—you could roast an ox before it!"
Then he turned and fled, leaving Roch over-
whelmed with vexation and astonishment.

"He must be mad!" she exclaimed. She
knelt down in front of the little pool and
looked at herself. "He must be mad!" she
repeated.

She glanced again at the pool. "Oh, I am
sure he's mad!" she added, in a more satisfied
voice. She took another little glimpse into
the pool. "There isn't the least doubt he's
mad!" she cried, exultantly. "Oh dear!"
she ended in a voice of dismay, her eyes
falling on a crushed box beneath the tree,
"there are the chocolates, and the Red-haired
Man has sat upon them!"

High up on the hill opposite she could see
the Red-haired Man tearing along with great,
wide-paced strides. She watched him a
moment. "He's rough and gauche," she exclaimed; "he's not a bit clever; he has
nothing that one really cares for or expects
to find in a man; he's an unlicked cub—and
yet——" she stopped short, and, returning to
the pool, knelt down once more, peering again
into its shadowy waters. "It would be very

strange if he should be the first man who did not think me beautiful," she said at length.

CHAPTER VII

THE sun beat hotly down on the hills round Olevano. Roch and the Red-haired Man had been gathering cyclamen, and, with hands and arms full of flowers, left the woods and sat down beneath the shadow of a rock. Down the rock's face, with a full-lunged gurgle, ran a stream, sending up a shower of spray which fell in beads on Roch's hair, making it crinkle up like a baby's tight-closed fist. Some distance from her mistress lay Felice, full in the sun, emitting from time to time a short pleased grunt of satisfaction as the genial warmth penetrated her black skin. The Red-haired Man had dropped his flowers into Roch's lap and flung himself down at her feet. He was supremely happy, and asked nothing more of life just then than to watch her deft, slim fingers rearranging the cyclamen. He had entered into that state of delight which at the same time arrests the mind and forces on it the impression that the faculties were never more keenly awake: he was certain that he had never lived, never come into full possession of himself, till that moment. Further than that he did not wish to analyse: possibly it may be a part of supreme happiness that we have neither the desire nor the capacity to analyse it.

The soft warm air blew between them. She raised her eyes and smiled at him, he smiled back at her: as a sensitive plant trembles at the far-off tramp of horses, their hearts thrilled at the unperceived approach of love. Neither had any thought of being untrue to Jess. Unconsciously they had stepped out of the cold land of thought into the warm land of emotion; and as he lay and watched the faint quiver of her gown above her bosom, it seemed to him that he embraced life and put his lips on happiness. Suddenly, subtly his gaze oppressed her. Springing to her feet, gathering the cyclamen together with both hands, she flung them full in his face. Shaking himself free from the flowers, he pursued her. She took shelter in the white cloud of spray, he following, and they stood there—the water

flashing in their hair and eyes, youth in their
hearts. High up on the mountain the great
horned cattle lowed to each other, and along
the steep path came the goats towards the
stream to drink. Roch and the Red-haired
Man, looking out across the valley, laughed
for sheer joy of living.

Unheeded by them, clouds had begun to
mass overhead; there was a dull, heavy clang
of thunder; in the far horizon the lightning
worried the sky. They turned and began to
retrace their steps towards the Albergo. The
rain overtook them, and they found shelter at
last in an empty reed-hut. Before the door
was an almond-tree in full bloom; a gust of
wind tore off its blossoms, and the little tree
bowed over the broken petals that were the
spoils of its own beauty.

Suddenly the sky ripped from end to end,
and over the brink a sea of flame rolled
down upon the mountain. The man and
woman shrunk together, and in that blaze
of light they read their own hearts. A sense
of separation fell on them both. In silence
they went out into the storm and returned
back again to the Albergo.

CHAPTER VIII

The sun was nearing its setting, when, some
days later, the Red-haired Man, with Pico
astride on his shoulders, made his way along
the narrow mountain-track. He walked
rapidly as if to out-distance his thoughts;
the tuneless, wavering whistle of the shepherd's pipes beat on the still air,—but he
heard no sound except the thud of his own
pulses. He did not even glance round when
a herd of big horned cattle swept across the
path at a lopping gallop. Only Pico crowed
loudly at the rush of their hoofs, at the
tossing of their majestic heads.

At last he stopped, and, having found a
soft green spot between the bracken for Pico,
flung himself down beside him. But the
baby crawled up to his accustomed place
on the broad chest, and, stretching out his
little fat legs, doubling his fist, beat a loud
tattoo, wishing perhaps to awaken the Red-
haired Man, who lay and stared dully into
the sky, oblivious to the wants of his small
friend.

".Ah, Pico, old man!" he said, as if in response to the thumps, "never try and set the world to rights. It doesn't pay, old man—it doesn't pay."

The baby crowed derisively. In his eyes the world was a very fine place indeed, and needed no setting to rights.

"Pico," continued the Red-haired Man, "I suppose it never happened to you not to know your own mind—not even when you cried for the moon?"

The baby snatched at a belated butterfly, paying no heed to such trivial questions.

"Pico, Pico," said the man, taking the baby's two little fat fists in one of his great hands, "let us talk things out. Truth is the very devil when we run away from it. You see, Pico," he continued, "it was like this. There was a woman——"

The baby pulled his hands free and turned his back at the mention of woman.

"You've a lot to learn yet, Pico," the Red-haired Man remonstrated,—"a lot to learn. Woman isn't quite a nonentity in this world, Pico—she's very much alive. Now, this one I was telling you about—life has been hard

14

down on her from the first, but she had
plenty of pluck : she put her back up against
the wall and faced it, till I came along and
mulled everything. A man doesn't like to
see a woman facing things too much, Pico;
he wants to stand up beside her and hit out.
You don't understand now, old fellow, but
you will understand right enough by and by.
Well, that's how I felt, only I thought there
was something more. It doesn't matter what
I thought, because, because——" he stopped
short, and the baby crowed and thumped his
friend's broad chest to emphasise approval of
the story.

"It was a dream," continued the Red-
haired Man,—"a damned dream," he ended
with a sob.

But Pico's dream at that moment was to
catch a big green beetle, so he crawled away
on his own account and the man flung himself on his face. "Dreams are hell," he cried
bitterly, "dreams are hell."

CHAPTER IX

On his way back to the Albergo the Red-haired Man met Jess. She was seated on a broken tree stump, near the spot where he had first told her of his love, and below him wound the stony path over which he had carried her. His thoughts were full of that scene; he seemed to hear his own voice repeating—" Tell me you are glad that you are lame," and her answer, " I am glad, glad ! " Looking at her, remembering all the love he had promised, of which he had now none left to give, nothing but the pity that she so despised, his heart ached for her and himself. She had been waiting for him, and when he stopped in front of her, and raised a troubled face to his, it seemed almost as if she had some dim prescience of the truth. He shuddered to think of the suffering such know'edge would entail on her sensitive proud nature, and told himself that, at all costs, it should be kept from her. Yet, with the inconsistency of weakness, he felt irritated at the greatness of her need of him, at her

weakness, at her love. "Why," he asked himself, "did she come to meet me?" Will she
always make a parade of her love in this
fashion?"

She scanned his face anxiously, trying to
interpret each change of expression. Her
scrutiny irritated him further—he turned
away to hide his annoyance. A quick pang
shot through her; she caught his hands.
"Have I vexed you?" she asked.

"Vexed! No," he answered, still keeping
his face averted.

"What is it?" she pressed. "I feel there
is something between us."

"Aren't you just a little difficult to
please?" he replied. The tone of his voice,
not the words, hurt her. His love meant so
much to her: but she had learnt to believe
in it lately; yet she had a sudden keen longing to reassure herself of its reality.

"It isn't that you love me any less?" she
asked. Her voice trembled, and something
in the tone of it went straight to the man's
heart. He turned to her, took both her
hands in his own. "I care for you more than
you think, Jess," he said, "and, perhaps," he

added under his breath, "more than I myself know." Her eyes filled with tears; she drew close to him and hid her face against his breast.

"Your love is so much to me," she sobbed. "At first I couldn't believe that you loved me, I seemed so different from the kind of women men love ; and now, if you took your love back, I would bear it, because it would be *you* who willed it back,—but oh, it would be hard, hard, hard."

He caressed her hair, and his voice shook with contrition. She fell to sobbing, as a child cries, short, broken, full-throated sobs, and he stroked her hair with his big awkward fingers ; but the nearness of her bosom to his gave him no thrill, and he comforted her coldly. Then Pico, who from his perch on the man's shoulders had peered down curiously at the weeping woman, set up a sudden odd little wail on his own account, and Jess, raising her face, held out her arms to the child. A subtle displeasure entered the man's heart —he drew back.

"Let me have him," she pleaded.

"No, no, he is too heavy for you."

"Oh, *give* him to me!" She stretched out her hands towards the child, as if she was stretching out her hands towards motherhood.

"No, no," he said, fiercely. It seemed to him that if she touched the child it would be sacrilege.

"Oh, *give* him to me!" she cried again; "the touch of his little hands would make our love seem less like a dream."

"Life is too real for dreams," he said, in a harsh, grating voice. He walked on towards the village, she limped after him; but each step he took made the distance between them greater.

She saw him give the child to its mother, and Pico borne into the house and the door closed. The Red-haired Man did not turn back to her, but strode off down the road. She covered her face with her hands. "It is a dream, a dream," she cried, bitterly; "he is beginning to awake."

And yet she could not believe it was a dream, even though she said it with her lips.

CHAPTER X

The villagers were returning from their day's work in the fields as the Red-haired Man hurried down the long grey road. He met groups of girls and lads chatting and laughing; a man on a mule ambled by, clasping in front of him a small child, while a boy perched behind the saddle gripped him tightly round the waist. Trudging after him came a woman, bearing in the basket on her head, which she steadied with one hand, her baby, who gazed out on the world in proud security of position. Through the little procession there ran the thread of natural human affection,—the affection that the Red-haired Man felt that he, with his own hands, was tearing out from the woof of his life. His heart swelled and protested bitterly against the sacrifice; the sight of the groups of peasants became hateful to him ; he broke away from them, jumped the hedge, and climbed up through an olive orchard towards the brow of the hill. When the trees hid him from sight he stopped, and putting his hands on a branch rested his face upon them. All day thought on thought had jarred one against the other in his mind; now his mind was empty of thought—his brain and heart had room for nothing but pain. The sweat broke out on his forehead. "For my whole life—for my whole life," he muttered —"I can't, I can't——" His agony drove him from the spot, and, hurrying through the orchard, he came to the farm-house. On the doorstep a woman sat nursing her child: for a moment he stood staring at her with so strange an expression on his face that the woman crossed herself involuntarily. Bursting into a wild, miserable laugh, he rushed on: suddenly he saw Roch in front of him. She was standing on the brow of the hill, looking out across the valley. He came and stood beside her: neither of them spoke; but the nearness of her presence quieted him, and thought began once more to flow in his brain. At last, as if by one accord, they turned and looked at each other: he saw that her face was no longer that of a child, but of a woman,—and when he marked the change, so much the more passionate became his need of her. He drew closer. "Come away with me," he said; "there is nothing in the whole world beside our love."

Despair swept down upon her: it was all so strange, sudden, terrible,—she was so unaccustomed to facing the stern realities of life. Involuntarily she raised her eyes to his, seeking help; but manliness had forsaken him. He laid his hands upon her breast: the touch of his hands burnt her like fire; but her bosom was to him womanhood, and the soft, fresh joys of the bridal night.

"Come," he said, "come, my beloved, you are mine; do I not possess you already?" and his hands slipped from her breast to her waist and soft rounded hips.

She sprang back, and stood trembling like a tall flame. Many moments went by—his passionate need of her rose in rebellion, protesting at her coldness. With a half articulate curse, he turned and left her.

CHAPTER XI

That evening the Red-haired Man did not return to the Albergo. When night fell Jess sat in the loggia waiting for him. At

the little shrine below Mad Gentia had lit
her candles in honour of the Madonna, and
in mute appeal to her pity; for Mad Gentia's
lover had lingered long far out at sea, and
the Blessed Mother of Christ remembering
this might hasten his return. Jess's heart
filled with pity, for she knew, as did all but
the mad woman, that the lover was drowned,
and would not return till the sea gave up
its dead. The candles burnt bravely, but
Gentia turned away, her heart beating high
with hope; then a sudden gust of wind blew
them out: but, after all, the man was drowned,
and even the Mother of God could not bring
a dead man to life. Still, be that as it may,
Jess rose from her seat, and, limping painfully
down the village steps, relit the candles.
Late that night, when the doors of the Albergo were fast shut and the Padrona and
her sons lay snoring heavily, Jess crept into
Roch's room. She shook her friend by the
shoulder: "He has not come back," she said.
"Why do you think he has not come back?"
Roch made no answer; and Jess, thinking
that she slept, left her. The days lengthened
into weeks, and the Red-haired Man did not

return. Every night fresh candles burnt before the little shrine: the villagers wondered openly where Mad Gentia got the money to buy so many candles, but Jess, sitting watching the spear-shaped flames, murmured to herself, " Who knows, he may come back tonight." At first Roch thought of the Red-haired Man's return with horror, then to the horror was added a great longing to see his face.

Jess had never spoken much to Roch about the Red-haired Man, but now it seemed that her heart was overburdened with words, and she was unwearied in telling of her faith in him and of his unshakeable fidelity : sometimes her voice clanged hard like steel, sometimes it shook with tears, but the theme of her talk in each case was the same,—for it was not Roch whom she worked to convince, but herself. Neither did Roch's feeling in listening vary, nor did she cease to shudder at each recurring of the word " faith."

One evening Roch sat upon her bed : her chestnut hair, unwound, looked like rusted gold against her white nightgown ; her small feet, crossed and pink, pressed the floor. Jess stood at the window, staring across the shadow-wrapt village at the little shrine.

"The candles have gone out," she exclaimed, suddenly.

"What candles?"

"Mad Gentia's——"

"Poor Gentia; but the man is dead."

"He is not dead," Jess answered, in a dreamy voice.

"Not dead? How do you know?"

"I cannot explain: Gentia knows; I know, —we feel it. You could not understand, Roch, because——" she stopped short, and then added gently, "When women love they learn these things."

Roch shivered. "Love is full of pain and horror," she said.

"No, no, no," replied Jess, putting out her hands protestingly; "love is most beautiful." She was silent a moment, and the white moonlight fell on her white face and figure,—her hair hung about her, soft like shadows.

"Listen, Roch," she said; "long ago, when you first knew me, I was hard, believed in no one: then I met him, and he loved me,"—

she was silent a moment. "I know," she continued, in a soft, hushed voice, "you think
that he will not come back to me, but, oh, I
am not afraid."

Roch flung herself face downwards on the
bed, and answered nothing.

All that night Roch lay awake: she did
not think, only suffered. The day dawned,
throwing white, then pale yellow, tints upon
the sky; but the earth beneath the mists
slept heavily. A fresh coolness fell upon
everything, and the bracken-covered hills
dripped dew. Faint, shuffling noises made
themselves heard, and one startled lark rose
straight upward, poising for a while on lev-
elled wings, then sinking back songless to
earth. Eastward, from behind a deeply dip-
ping mountain, the sun, slowly at first, and
then with a great smooth sweep, took its place
above the horizon. The goatherds unfastened
the pens, and the goats leapt and butted down
the steep mountain paths. Olevano itself
awoke; men, women, and children came out
into the streets, singly at first, then in groups;
the copper cans clanged at the well, and the

lichen-stained houses echoed back the patter of the unshod feet of mules. After a while Roch rose, dressed herself, and went out. It was her last day in Olevano: she was to leave by the early diligence, and join her mother in Rome,—Jess had refused to leave Olevano.

At the corner of the street she saw Pico: taking him from his mother, she carried him in her arms up the narrow winding paths that led away from the village out on to the hills. She came at last to the small pool in whose waters the Red-haired Man had first seen her beauty: beside the pool the Red-haired Man lay asleep. Roch stood watching him,—his face was worn with much suffering. The freshness of the morning stirred Pico's heart, —he crowed loudly. The Red-haired Man moved in his sleep, woke, saw Roch with the baby pressed close against her breast, and thought that he dreamed; but Pico struggled down from the girl's arms, crawled away, chuckling loudly, for he had been awake an hour or more.

On the loose stones of the mountain path there was the sound of a slow, halting tread: as it fell on the man's ears he awoke hurriedly, and fell back behind the, shelter of the trees. At the bend of the hill above Jess limped slowly into sight. He felt no surprise; it was as if he had been waiting for her. Each halting step that she took forward entered his heart like a knife. For a while Jess stood looking at the broken path; then it seemed that her courage failed her, and, turning, she went back the way she had come. The echo of her footsteps died; Roch and the Red-haired Man stood and stared each into the other's white face.

"She must never know," they stuttered hoarsely, "she must never learn the truth."

A great haste to be away came to the man—a great fear lingering.

"I will go to her," he said; "but you—we must never meet again."

"No," Roch answered, dully, "we must never meet again."

"The diligence—you can leave Olevano to-day."

His haste bruised her like stones. "Yes, I leave Olevano to-day."

"You must never write."

"No, I must never write."

"And if we meet you in the street you must not know us."

"If I meet you in the street I must not know you."

"Swear!" he said, turning from her.

"I swear."

Then he fled hurriedly, and she, raising Pico in her arms, pressed the baby close up against her breast—for upon her there was a lust of motherhood.

THE STONE PINE

15

THE STONE PINE

THEY dwelt beside the mulberry-shadowed Mediterranean, and were goatherds: he, a bare-legged, ragged boy; she, a short-kilted maiden in an olive green petticoat and blue blouse, faded and stained. Each day at ebb-tide they drove their flock along the shore that they might gather what the sea had cast aside,—for the goats had a keen appetite, and scarce anything came amiss to them. In front of the flock the boy walked, playing upon his reed pipe; the girl tripped content in the rear. He never turned back and looked on her, but talked to his pipe, or fell listening when it told him of the men's thoughts and deeds. As for the maid, she knitted her stocking, and was content, for she was but nine summers old, and felt scant curiosity about herself or him. The goats, too, needed a watchful eye,—there was the "Devil with the thousand Tricks" which

227

strayed away, and the " Weary One " that
ever lagged behind and needed much herd-
ing.   Now the "Devil with the thousand
Tricks" made the boy laugh: he would
punish it, fight with it and feel strong; but
for the " Weary One " he had nothing but
contempt, calling it feeble-couraged and a
woman.   The maid, however, loved it; but
the kid grew thin, do what she would.   At
night the goats were penned, and the boy
and girl slept beside them in a reed hut,
conical-shaped, with a small picture of the
Blessed Virgin nailed above the door, and
on the roof a curious prickly arrangement
to keep away witches—for who knew whether
with fall of sun strange things might be
abroad ?. Even the boy was sometimes afraid,
and would permit his small companion to
creep close to him and be comforted.   She
was grateful, as became her, holding his hand
long after he had dropped off to sleep, while
without the black and silent night seemed
ever about to speak and spoke not.

On the shore there grew a Stone Pine: it
was taller than all other pines, and as solitary
as God.   Even when the children and goats

lay close by, still it remained solitary; and
at rise and set of sun the red stem would
glow like a soul: fear would fall on the
children, and, rising, they would stand before
it with bent heads.   Sometimes the girl
wondered on the loneliness of the pine:
was it God-lonely from being above men,
their thoughts and ways?   The boy had
other thoughts, caring little for the pine, his
mind dwelling on curious bladed knives,
horses, and lands far out at sea, wreck-be-
girdled, and untrod by the foot of man. Yet
there were moments when he also tasted of
loneliness and felt brief fellowship with the
Pine; moments when the beauty of all the
earth seemed ripe, but in the harvest something lacking, though he knew not what it
was, neither had met any one who could
name it by name, the Pine also remaining
silent.   The years passed—the boy, reaching
up towards manhood, becoming good to look
on, so that when the maid walked behind the
flock she ceased to gaze down on her knitting,
but looked always at him. He did not glance
back at her, because the whole wide world
lay before him : besides, he had known her

from a child, and, let her strive much or little,
nothing but womanhood awaited her, a poor
state of scant account.

One day a great restlessness fell upon the
boy, so that taking his pipe he strayed away,
leaving the girl and flock alone. It was vint-
age time: men and maids pressed the stain-
ing grape with quick-paced feet, and he stood
and played to them while the purple juice
frothed in the old brown wooden vats. His
heart quickened, and drove him from them,
seeking satisfaction elsewhere. Climbing the
mountains, he passed white oxen dragging
blocks of marble. A sweet scent hung about
the beasts, so that he lingered a moment,
before pressing on, to look at their heavy
dewlaps and big luminous eyes.

Later he came to a seaport, and sailed that
evening in one of the feluccas. The west
wind blew upon him soft and fragrant, and
bore with it the scent of other lands, and his
heart waxed impatient for the sight of them.
Many weeks passed, and the felucca coasted
slowly down the Mediterranean, then ported
helm, and began to sail as slowly back.
Sometimes the boat lay becalmed, and all on

board except the boy slept beneath the
shadow of the brown sail: he alone was glad
when the breeze sprang up once more, and
the waves leapt like a laugh against the bows.
Sometimes, too, they would drop anchor at
strange ports; the sailors would go ashore
and drink their fill of red wine and of the
red lips of girls: but such scenes moved the
boy little, though his heart did not cease to
burn restlessly.

Then one day, the felucca having reached
its journey's end, the sails were clewed up,
and the boy was free, if he would, to return
home. The sun lay low upon the horizon
when he drew near and saw the maid seated
beneath the shadow of the Stone Pine. She
rose to her feet, and they stood and looked at
each other: he saw that she was beautiful,
and the restlessness left his heart, so that he
wondered.

A great fear fell on them both: the maid
turned and fled, he following,—though why
she fled, or why he, who could have overtaken
her, did not, neither of them knew.

Then at last her knees trembled, and she
ran back to the Pine for shelter. But when

the boy saw that she was afraid, he grew bold, took her in his arms, and kissed her on the lips—the Pine beside them glowing like a soul.

THE STORM

THE STORM

A SUDDEN gale had sprung up from the north-east; great black-backed gull and feeble-winged puffin had been forced alike through the smoking mists inland. Night fell amid the clash of wind and sea. A narrow track winding round the cliffs led past a cottage; light shone from the windows, and in the kitchen were three women. The youngest lay in a truckle bed, a baby against her breast; an old woman, tall, gaunt, and white-haired, sat at a table, the Bible before her, muttering over familiar passages with awkward lips; the third moved softly about the room preparing supper. She stood a moment by the bed, as the child broke into a long, low wail.

"Poor lamb!" she said; "he frets as if your breast was cold to him."

"Maybe 'tis cold," replied the sick girl, indifferently.

"Ay, but not to-night, Nan," the other protested, "and his father out in a storm like this!"

"The Lord have mercy on the lad!" exclaimed the old woman, glancing up; "he's got that scamp Rab Tapp wi' him in the boat. Scores o' times I've told Joss 'twould be safer to sail 'long o' decent folk."

Nan stirred uneasily. "Rab's as good as the rest o' 'em," she muttered, "and a long ways handier."

"Handy wi' his tongue belike," retorted the old woman; "there ain't his equal for lying in this here parish. 'Tis only reasonable that the Lord should be angered agin him; though maybe the Almighty will mind that Joss has been a good son to me, and spare the boat."

She was silent a moment, listening to the continuous clamour of the massive door-bolts that barred back the storm. "Ay, that Rab," she burst out, fiercely, "they should cast him overboard the same as the men o' Joppa cast the prophet Jonah, son of Amittai. Who knows but the Almighty may be speaking now by the voice o' the wind—'Cast him out, cast him out, and the raging waves of the sea shall foam upon his shame.'"

"How dare 'ee speak such words as them!" cried the girl, springing up in bed. "The Lord ain't no Moloch to devour men's lives."

"And what's Rab Tapp's life to thee?" replied the other, sternly. "It ill becomes a mother with her first chile at breast to be taking such thought for furren men's lives."

"Come, come, mother," interposed the third woman, "let Nan be: supper's on the table, and you'd feel better for a snatch o' sommat."

"I did well to name 'ee Martha," cried the old woman, turning on her. "Your thoughts be too much taken up wi' the things o' this world. What call have I for bite or sup when the great starved sea is hungering after my son? Ay, but Joss, lad, lad," she continued to herself, "and you that fond o' whistling!"

Martha made no answer, but, pouring out a cup of tea, brought it to the sick girl. "Happen 'twill quench your thirst a bit, Nan," she said.

"'Tain't that kind o' thirst," replied the other, wearily.

" Take it all the same, lass," Martha urged ;
and the girl drank.

" 'Tis salt as the sea ! " she exclaimed, pushing the cup from her with a shudder. " Seems
as if I knowed the taste o' drowning."

" And well you may," exclaimed the old
woman, " when your man is forced so nigh
to it."

" Joss will not be drowned," replied her
daughter-in-law carelessly. " What-for should
he be drowned? Oh, my God ! " she ended,
with abrupt change of voice, as the hurrying
scream of the storm wrenched its way through
the cottage, " why did yer make the sea ? "
She flung herself back in the bed, and the
child began once more to cry, but she paid
no heed to it.

" Poor heart ! " said Martha, stooping and
raising the baby in her arms, " he frets over
things." She walked to and fro in the little
kitchen, her face pressed close against the
child's, her soft brown hair mingling with his
soft downy fluff. " My own chile," she continued meditatively, " was wonderful con-
tentsome."

" Your own chile ! " exclaimed the harsh-voiced old woman. "Why, your own chile was born dead."

"Her was never dead to me," Martha answered, gently. "I used to talk a deal to her lying there so close and trustful agin my heart. But now I sorter feel that if me and Jim had another chile, maybe 'twould be born dead."

"Ay, and no wonder," retorted her mother; "a more shiftless body than Jim I ain't come across—always trapesing round in searching work and never finding it. He's a poor stick; the sea never gave him no call, and you can sit here and eat your victuals content, come storm, come clear."

The sick girl raised herself on her arm. "There's one thing I never could fathom," she exclaimed with sudden interest, "and that's his being own brother to Rab. Why, he ain't no patch on him!"

"No," rejoined her mother-in-law, sharply; "he's more fool than cheat, for certain. If 'twor he out in the boat wi' Joss, happen the Lord might overlook him."

The girl's dark eyes flashed, and Martha interposed, in a hurt voice, "Maybe Jim ain't so quick at the take up as Rab; but he's mortal persevereshous at trying. After all, Nan," she added, "you ain't never seen Rab but twice."

"No, I ain't never seen him but twice," the girl repeated.

"And when ye did meet never spoke much to one 'nother!" continued Martha, wonderingly.

"No, us never spoke much to one 'nother."

"Ay, certain," exclaimed Martha; "why, the last time he comed in here 'twas a matter of three weeks ago; you was sitting up in front of the fire nursing the chile, and he just stood over again 'ee by the chimney-piece, sorter thoughtful. 'Do you love it?' he axed, 'do you love it?'—but you didn't make no answer. Them were his words. Do you mind, Nan?"

"Yes," said the girl, softly, "I mind."

"'Twas a queer question I reckoned to put to a mother; but there, you ain't never been terrible took up wi' the chile."

"No."

"Maybe you didn't speak to him sorter

tender afore you borned him—same as I did my little girl."

" No."

" Yet 'twor my chile that wor born dead."

" Ay," the girl answered, fiercely, "and ain't mine born dead too ? "

The elder woman glanced at her in astonishment. " What ails you, Nan ? " she exclaimed. " Why, the poor lamb is calling for the breast."

" I don't hear it call," the girl answered, stonily.

Martha looked down with sad eyes at the child on her knee. " You don't love it terrible tendersome," she said.

The girl, turning away her head, made no reply. Without the storm clamoured more fiercely, and the faces of the listening women grew white and tense. " Pray for them at sea," exclaimed Martha, glancing at her mother.

" And ain't I praying for 'em ? " expostulated the old woman, passionately.

" Say the words aloud, mother, and let us join in."

The old woman clasped her hands, worn
16

with toil, knotted with age, and sank on her
knees; her thin lips trembled, but no words
broke from them. Wind and sea, as if in
derision at her helplessness, burst into more
hideous combat, and the thunder heaved its
way through their clamour with a noise like
the splitting of mountains.

"O God!" sobbed the woman, "he wor a
good son to me—a good son to me." She
was silent a moment, and the storm without
upreared itself against the cliffs, rocking the
cottage in its heavy embrace. "O God!"
she burst forth again, "ye would have spared
Sodom for the sake of ten righteous men, and
'twor a terrible big and wicked city—spare
the boat cause o' Joss! I wouldn't have
axed so bold if it wor a ship; but it's nought
but a boat, mortal small and tiddleliwinkie,
wi' only dree men an' a lad in it; and the
lad's a decent lad come o' respectable church
folk, no chappelites, a-setting o' theirselves
up above their betters. Happen you're angered again Rab Tapp, and well you might
be, for he's not over and above conspicuous
in good works; still, he's young, and youth's
larning time: but, if ye be terrible set on

cutting him off—and I'll not deny the temptation—then, O Lord God! speak to Joss through the mouth o' the winds, same as ye did the men o' Joppa, so that he shall rise and cast Rab forth into the deep, and the sea shall cease her raging."

As she uttered the last words the sick girl sprang from the bed and caught the old woman by the shoulders. "How dare 'ee mind the Almighty o' Rab's weaknesses at such a time!" she cried, passionately.

"And do you reckon that the Lord has forgotten 'em?" replied the old woman, in a hard voice. "Ain't they all written in the Book o' Judgment?"

"There be scores and scores o' folk on the sea to-night," the girl answered, "deal wickeder folk than Rab, and why should the Almighty be special took up wi' he? Oh, 'twas cruel, cruel of yer to put Him in mind o' the lad!"

"Ain't the names o' all sailor men written on the same page, that the Lord may read and choose in the winking o' an eye? And shall I see my own son cast away for fear o' speaking out?" remonstrated the old woman, fiercely. "My first-born, that lay at my breast and milked me trustsome? Shame on you to think o' stranger folk afore your own wedded husband."

While she spoke there was the sound of heavy knocking on the door without. Martha crossed the room, shot back the great bolts, and a man, pale-faced, drenched, and battered, staggered in. The old woman gave an abrupt, keen cry. "My son!" she exclaimed, and would have taken him in her arms, but he put her gently aside and came towards the girl, who stood barefooted on the cold stone floor, her long brown hair curling over her coarse night-gown.

"Nan," he cried, "sweetheart, woman, wife, God's given me back to 'ee!"

"And Rab?" she said, hoarsely.

"The sea has taken its toll—Rab's drowned," he answered.

"'Twas he I loved!" she cried, and fell at the man's feet as dead.

AT THE STROKE OF THE HOUR

AT THE STROKE OF THE HOUR

IT was Christmas Eve, the snow lay thick on the village street, the waits were out, and small children sat up in bed feeling very happy, though they did not well know why. But Sam Crag, sitting alone in his cottage, did not feel happy. Fifty years had he been clerk-sexton in the parish church, and now he was to be clerk-sexton no more; therefore the world seemed to him a sorry place, and Christmas out of joint. Fifty dull, stiff-jointed, yawnful years; but they had not seemed long to Sam Crag, and it was the death of the rector that first brought home to him that he too had lagged behind his time. The supposition pained him, and he fought against it, for his sap of obstinacy had not yet run dry. Crag had always spoken of the rector and himself as " us two "; and for years " us two " had managed the little, out-of-the-way country parish much as they had wished.

The new rector was a young man, not without ideas, and determined among other things to restore the church, sweep away the high-backed pews and creaky galleries, and Sam Crag along with them.

In the village there were certain almshouses known as the Bede cottages. The occupiers of these cottages received a weekly dole of half-a-crown and a quartern loaf of bread. The bread was often heavy, and apt to contain foreign substances not previously recognised as nutritious; but then, as the baker said, "It was a charity loaf, and good for such," though in a moment of unusual expansiveness he had been known to add, "that they who set out to live on charity had best look to their teeth."

When the rector had told Crag that he had grown too old for his work, he had told him also that he was to have a vacant Bede cottage, the weekly half-crown and quartern loaf of bread. Nothing, therefore, seemed more certain than that life for him was to be shorn of all care, and that he might totter to the grave without fear of starving by the way; but Crag, with the strange ingratitude

of the poor, had declared he would have
" none o' their charities," and when remonstrated with had cursed the new rector to his
face for " a snip of a currit."

So it had come about that sorrow on this
Christmas Eve laid a heavy hand on Crag,
and his ears had grown deaf to the song of
the waits. Now, sitting in the corner of his
kitchen, his eyes fell suddenly on the massive
church keys. He rose and unhooked them
from the nail behind the door—the nail on
which, each Sunday night, they had come
back to rest till the following Saturday, when
the church was unlocked and cleaned. They
had grown used to that nail, and the nail to
them, for the Crags, father and son, had been
clerk-sextons for three generations.

It was at this moment that a knock sounded
on the door and a man entered : he looked at
Crag with a mixture of curiosity and pity.

" I've come," he said, " for the keys."

Crag made no attempt to give them to him,
but stood turning them over and over in his
hand,—his chest heaved, and a tear splashed
through the clumsy wards on to the floor.

" I've knowed 'em," he exclaimed, " ever

since I was a chile." The man's face grew
red. He looked first at Crag, then at the
keys, and after a moment's hesitation turned
on his heel and went out.

"I reckon," he muttered, "'twould be as
well to call termarrer."

After a while Crag, having locked his cottage door, made his way slowly through the
village street, and up the hill where the church
stood sentinel above the dead.

Entering, he went to where, in a corner of
one of the crypts, he kept his shovel and pick,
and having taken them passed out of church
again. He climbed over the rugged graves
till he reached an elm-tree, at the foot of
which his wife lay buried. Forty years she
had lain there, her baby at her breast—
he had placed them in one coffin. "Her'll
sleep quieter so," he said, and she had never
stirred, but still slept on.

It had been on Christmas Eve that she had
died: he remembered that night well—the
snow lay on the ground, and the moon shone
full. The waits had been singing a Christmas
hymn, and she had told him to open wide the
window that she might hear more clearly, for

the deafness of death was upon her. He had
done so, and the words—

"Peace on earth, and mercy mild,
God and sinners reconciled,"

floated in through the falling snow, and she,
hearing them, smiled and passed out to meet
Him in whose praise they sang.

Crag cleared the snow away from the
patch of ground next to his wife's grave,
and then began to dig. It seemed to him
that, somewhere in his dulled brain, two
voices spoke, and one said, "Whose grave is
this?"

And the other answered, "Wait and you
will know all."

Then Loony Jack, the village idiot, came
and peered down upon him. A strange fool
was Loony Jack, and some there were who
said that he had the power of scenting death
afar off. He watched the old man pick and
shovel, shovel and pick, and then burst into
a laugh, wild, mocking, miserable; but Crag
heeded him not, for now he knew that it was
his own grave he dug, and he desired to dig
it well. Loony Jack got tired of watching

and went his way, but the echo of the laugh
lingered among the graves. At last Crag
finished his work and returned once more to
the church, and as he shut the door behind
him his left hand fumbled restlessly with the
handkerchief around his neck; a moment
later and he had untied it. Passing between
the high-backed pews he came to the altar,
and stood there, drawing the handkerchief
through his fingers, backwards and forwards.
It was at those same altar-steps that he, one
morning in May, had knelt to be married;
and now the memory of that day came back
to him again. Once more he saw himself rise
at dawn, and steal hand in hand with her, who
so soon was to be his bride, across the quiet
fields, where the blue mist hung sleepily.
There, with none but the sky to see them,
they had made a daisy chain. His part had
been to kiss the daisies, hers to weave the
flowers. The chain woven, she hung it
around his hat, for a lad must needs look
his best upon his wedding morning. Then
they had stolen home, to meet again before
the altar of the old church and swear to
love and cherish each other till Death did

them part. And Death had parted them; but now, he said to himself, Death should bring them together again. The clock in the tower gave a great whirring scream, preparatory to striking the hour.

"I'll do it on the stroke o' the hour," muttered the old man—"on the stroke o' the hour."

He wound the handkerchief round his neck, his eyes still filled with visions of his dead wife. Young and fair she seemed to him, and he himself felt like a lad going to meet his bride. Then there came to him the knowledge that between the death that she he loved had died, and that which he would bring upon himself, there was a great gulf fixed. Thinking of it, he fell upon his knees. "Oh, God," he sobbed, "is the difference so mortal great, so mortal great?"

From out of the gloom of the church a voice answered, "Blessed are the dead that die in the Lord."

For one awful moment the old man rose to his feet, then swayed, and fell forward on his face. Through the church rang peal after peal of discordant laughter. Loony Jack was

playing at funerals; but Crag heeded him
not, for he was dead.

Then with a whir the clock tolled twelve,
and Christmas Day dawned upon the world.

TRAVELLING JOE

TRAVELLING JOE

IT was Sunday: the mill was silent, and the water pressed idly against the big dam, opposite which stood old Zam Tapp's cottage. Zam was seated in the dark kitchen, a bucket of water between his knees, peeling potatoes; and lying in a truckle-bed was his grandson Travelling Joe, a boy of about nine years old, small, wizen, and partly paralysed. The tall clock in the corner of the room had struck twelve, and groups of people passed the cottage on their return from church and chapel. Zam, who did not "howld wi' zich things," eyed them with indifference, not unmixed with contempt. He "reckoned," he said, "thet ha didn't want no praicher to teach him tha way tu 'eaven; zalvation wez a kooris thing, and, like cream, let it alone and twid come to 'ee: meddle and praying widn't fetch it."

To the boy lying there, his heart full of

the spirit of adventure, and his life bounded
by the truckle-bed and the four walls of the
small kitchen, the thought of heaven was of
piercing interest; it haunted his dreams sleeping and waking, it was his New America, the
land which he would one day explore.   To
him it never ceased to be a matter of regret
that the Crystal Sea lay in front of the
throne of God; he would have wished it
might have been in what he called the " *dimmet* [1] part o' 'eaven* "; a far border-land un-
known to the angels, and where even the eye
of God fell seldom.   And now as he lay and
watched Zam peeling the potatoes, he longed
unconsciously to hear the " loosing of the
mill," for the sound of the great waters leap-
ing forth was to him as the rushing of the
River of Life.

Zam's mind was occupied by the thought of
his dead wife. " Eh! eh! " he exclaimed,
suddenly, " hur wez a windervul 'and at biling
a tetty, wez my owld wuman, and when it
coomed tu tha last hur mind dwelt on it
painvul. 'Vather,' hur zed, 'I reckon I've
cooked 'ee my last tetty.' 'I reckon 'ee 'ave,

[1] Dusky, dim, full of shadows.

moather,' I answered. Hur wez zilent a bit,
then all-ta-wance hur zot up in bed and
ketched howldt o' me by tha weskit. 'Tull
Jane'—thic wez yer pore moather—'tull
Jane,' hur zed, 'twez tha zalt thet did it;
twez all along o' tha zalt.' But, law bless
'ee, zalt or no zalt, Jane's tetties wez niver
a patch on hurn. I reckon hur hand will
ba moast out o' biling tetties by tha time I
jines hur; but law, I doant complain, moast
like tez zweet stuff they lives on up ther:
I niver cud stomach zich stuff mezulf; but
bless 'ee, glory hez tu be paid for the same ez
tha rest."

A vision of his grandmother's portly form
arose in the child's mind as he lay and listened. "Grandfer," he said, "do 'ee reckon
thet grandmoather took tu wings natrel fust
along?"

Zam stopped peeling the potatoes. "Many's
tha time I've thought on thic, Joe," he answered, sorrowfully, "and I ba moast a-feardt
hur didn't; tha noo-fangled ways wez alwiz
contrary tu hur, and if ther wez wan thing
more than a tother hur cudn't abide twez
a loose veather in her bed. Eh! eh! I wid

dearly o' liked tu o' gone along fust and put hur in tha way o' things a bit; but ther, if yer doant lave things tu tha Almighty, who shall 'ee leave 'em to?"

"Tha Laurd ba turribul mindful o' poor folk," the boy said, questioningly.

"Ay, ay, lad," the old man answered, "ther ba a deal o' tha wuman about tha Almighty. Ha wull pramise 'ee an ill tarn if yer doant mend; but Ha ba zlow tu lay it on—zlow tu lay it on."

Joe was silent a moment, and Zam began once more to peel the potatoes. At last the boy spoke. "Sposing grandmoather wez tu break her wing," he cried, excitedly, "what then, grandfer—what then?"

The old man flushed. "Angels baint for doing zich things ez thic, Joe," he answered; "there's nought promiscuous in 'eaven. I reckon thet they thet ba noo tu tha trade flies mortal zlow fust along—zummat like owld Varmer Rod's payhen; no hitting o' theirselves agin a tray. Yer grandmoather kind o' thought o' thic hurzulf, and jest avor hur turned over in hur bed for tha last time, her looked up in me vace kind o' trustzome,

'I'll take it aisy, vather,' her zed, 'and the Laurd wull do the rast.' 'Eh! eh! moather,' I zed, 'Ha woant forzake 'ee. Ha's bin a pore man Hiszulf, an' knaws what tiz not tu ba larned.' Hur smiled, but I zaw tha tears in hur eyes. 'I shall miss yer hand, vather,' hur zed, 'tha valley o' tha shader ba turribul dark.' 'The Laurd wull walk wi' 'ee, moather,' I zed, 'Hiz hand ba more restful than mine.' 'Eh, but vust along,' her murmured, 'vust 'long'; then hur claused hur eyes and died quietvul. Hur wez mortal much a duman, poor zoul. Conzarvitive to tha end—conzarvitive to tha end."

Later, when the frugal dinner had been cooked and eaten, Zam drew his big arm-chair up to the fire and fell asleep. The boy closed his eyes too, but only that he might the more easily dwell in an imaginary world. He wondered what the far confines of heaven looked like, and whether he should find volcanoes there, and as he pictured the scene he suddenly startled the old man out of his sleep. "Grandfer, grandfer," he cried excitedly, "sposing 'eaven shid blaw up!"

"Bless tha boy," Zam answered, looking

anxiously at the small fire, "I thought vor zure tha kettle wez biling auver."

"Naw, granfer," said Joe, "I wez only a-wondering what tha dimmet parts o' 'eaven might be arter when God wez kind o' thinking o' zommat ulse."

Zam's deep-set eyes twinkled. "A bit contrary may ba," he said, "but nought light-zome, Joe—nought lightzome."

"Folk ba turribul spiritless up tu 'eaven," the boy answered, sadly. "They baistesses now that stand avor tha throne—do 'ee reckon thet they iver roar?"

"Wull," his grandfather answered after a moment, "I widn't reckon on it, if I wez you, Joe—I widn't reckon on it; but," he added, as his eyes fell upon the boy's disappointed face, "who can tull what the talking o' zich critters as thic wull be like—fearsome, no doubt."

"And, grandfer," Joe exclaimed, with rising colour, "if lame Tom wez ther wi' hiz crutch now, and jest stepped on tha taw o' wan o' they baistesses, then ha wid talk mortal spiritty, grandfer, widn't ha?"

"Eh, for zure, for zure, mortal spiritty, I'll be bound," Zam answered.

The flush of excitement died out from the boy's face. "Moast like 'twull niver happen," he said, in a sorrowful voice; "up tu 'eaven things ba painful riglar."

"Ba 'ee tired, lad?" Zam asked, as he rose from his chair and lifted the child tenderly in his arms. "Shall I carry 'ee tu and fraw a bit?"

Joe pressed his thin white face against the old man's breast.

"Tull me about things avor I wez born, grandfer," he said. "Tull me about vather; wez ha vine and upstanding?"[1]

"Ay, ay, lad, ha wez pleasant tu look upon," Zam answered, "but ha brauk yer pore mother's heart for all o' thic. He wez turribul wild, wez Jim; good-hearted anuff, but turribul wild; ha wezn't built for marrying; ha cudn't stay pauking about in a little vullage zich ez this ba; ha zed thet tha wordel wez zmall anuff, but ez vor tha village, ha couldn't breathe in it; and yer pore moather hur cudn't get tu understand thet nohow—hur reckoned thet if ha loved hur, ha wud stay; but, law bless 'ee, lad, vor men zich ez Jim

[1] Well built.

ther ba zommat ulse in the wordel beside tha
love o' women-folk, tho' they, pore zouls, cant
gaw fur tu zee it. But ha wez turribul fond
o' hur vor all thic, and I cud zee thet it jest
went tu his heart tu act contrary; but ha
cudn't help it, pore lad—twez the nater thet
wez in him fo'ced him on. Eh, but they made
a windervul handzome couple tha day they
wez merrid; the vullage riglar tarned out tu
look on 'em, and I thort tu mezulf thet twid
o' bin a proud day vor my pore owld wuman
if tha Almighty had spared hur; but twez
better ez it twez—better ez it wez. Wull,
they hadn't a-bin merrid a skaur o' wiks avore
Jim wez riglar pining tu ba off: ha didn't
zay nought, but wid gaw and wander about
in tha wids for haurs, and wan day ha didn't
coome 'ome; he wrote from Liverpool tu zay
ha wez starting vor Merikey. But tha ship
wez lost wi' all 'ands; ay, ay, pore lad, I
reckon ha zlapes zound anuff now wi' tha
zay a-rolling a-tap o' him: ha cud niver o'
breathed iv it had bin airth. But yer
moather, hur niver forgave him vor it—niver:
twez a Zunday thet tha noos coomed, and
Martha Snykes and zome o' tha naybours

rinned up yhere ez fast ez they cud, pore
zouls, reckoning thet yer moather wid like to
cry all-tugether comfortabul, tha zame ez it
iz uyshil wi' wimen; but, law bless 'ee, when
her saw they well-maining dumans cooming
droo tha door, hur tarned hur back quat[1] on
'em and marched up-stairs. Arter a bit her
coomed down wi' a bonnet all auver pink roses
atap o' hur 'ead, and Martha Snykes wez thet
tooked aback thet hur fell down wi' tha recurring spasams and drank ivery drop o' brandy
ther wez in the 'ause avor hur wez brought to.
Yer moather didn't throw a look at hur,
but went off down tha strait tu charch wi'
all tha naybours standing at ther doors and
crying shame; but, law bless 'ee, hur didn't
heed 'em ony more than tha geese on tha
green. Ay, ay, pore zoul, hur wez alwiz
wan for howlding hur head high; hur niver
cud stomach tha contrary. Wull, wull,
women's women, mortal strong in tha af-
fections, but managing tu tha last—managing tu tha last. Them wez turribul days,
and yer moather's vace grew that hard I wez
moast afeardt tu look at it. I thought mayba

[1] Plump

thet when yer coomed things might o' bin diffurrent; I tooked 'ee in tu hur. 'Jane,' I zed, 'ha wull want 'ee alwiz,' and when I zed thic hur kained[1] acrass at 'ee, and hur vace changed back intu a wuman's vace agin; then all-ta-wance zommat coomed auver hur and hur tarned hur vace round agin tha wall. 'Take 'im away,' hur zed, 'ha ba nought tu me.' Hur niver spoke arter thic; ther wez ony wan pusson in the wordel thet hur iver loved, and thet wez Jim, and when ha died, hur wi' all hur pride wez fo'ced tu valler."

Later, when Zam laid the boy in the old truckle-bed, Joe looked up in his face. "Vather wez mortal understandabul," he murmured sleepily.

"But not tu women-folk," Zam answered, "not tu women-folk. Wull, wull," he continued to himself, "tha lad hez hiz vather's spirut, ivery bit o' it; but ha wull niver break no wuman's heart wi' wandering,—tha Lord hez minded otherwise."

.   .   .   .   .   .

It was about a week after the conversation recorded had taken place that Joe's uncle,

[1] Looked intensely.

Ben Tapp, came to Zam's cottage; but the old man was not at home, and Ben, who, after many years spent in America, had arrived in England only to find that most of his relations were dead and he himself forgotten, sat down on Travelling Joe's bed in an exceedingly bad humour with himself and the world in general.

"Wall, Travelling Joe," he said, "thet be a darned queer start o' a name yer have fixed to yerself anyhow. They pins o' yars ain't extra spry at covering the ground, I shud think from the look o' 'em."

"But things wull ba mortal diffurent up ta 'eaven, uncle Ben," the boy answered. "Ther woant ba no diffurence 'twixt me and tother folk then, 'cept mayba I shall ba more rasted. I shall do a sight o' travelling when I gets up ther; you zee, uncle Ben, tha Almighty ba powerful understandzome, zo I ain't got no cause tu ba feardt when I gaws up avore tha throne, and I shall jest ax Him tu let me vind noo ways droo tha dimmet parts o' 'eaven. 'Dear Laurd,' I shall zay, 'I knaws what rasting ba like, and now I wid dearly like tu ba doing.'"

Just as Ben Tapp would have tortured any helpless animal that fell into his power, so now, as he looked down on the boy's eager, pathetic face, a desire came into his heart to crush out its happiness.

"Thar ain't no such place as 'eaven, Joe," he said, leaning forward and placing his great hand on the child's cripple form; "'tis all darned rot—bunkum, as us says out in the States. And as for the Almighty that yer talk so slick about, tha bally old 'oss has kicked his last kick. Natur hez played low down on yer, Joe, and tied yer up to yar darned bed; but when Death gits hould of yer, ha wull tie yer a tarnation sight tighter, yer can bet yer bottom dollar on thet, Joker;" and the man burst into a laugh of coarse en-joyment. "Thar, young shaver," he added, as he rose from the bed, "thet's the opinion o' wan thet has covered a darned sight more miles in his life than yer have minutes, so stow it in yar pipe and smoke it": so saying, he left the child alone. But from that mo-ment a change came over Travelling Joe—he began to pine away, and the villagers said he was "marked for death"; but Zam, as he walked to and fro with the dying boy in his arms, muttered, " Better death than thet tha Union shid 'ave him; better thet than thic— better thet than thic."

One day, when it was plain that Joe was more than usually ill, Martha Snykes came to the cottage. " I jest drapped in, Zam Tapp," she said, sinking her stout form in the near-est chair, "to tull 'ee o' a remedy, a mortal efficumcasious remedy, tho' I zay it ez shudn't, baing, zo tu spake, the inventor o' tha zame. But, law, I've suffered thet turribul bad me-zulf; what wi' tha recurring spasams, and a percussion in the head that jest drones on con-tinuel for all the wordel like the passon o' praiching o' Zundays, thet I caut a-bear tu think of the pore child wi' death rampaging auver him, and tha cure, zo tu spake, at hiz vurry door; tha zame baing nort ulse but a tayspoonful o' tha brownest o' sugar, togither wi' a tayspoonful o' tha strongest o' brandies, and let it be tooked zitting, Natur liking a smoothness at zich times. I have alwiz reckoned mezulf thet if thet child's moather had vallered my advice and tooked thickey remedy, hur wid niver 'ave bin lying in tha

charchyard at this yhere blessid minnit ; tho'
I won't gaw for tu deny thet hur made a vine
corpse, straight vaychers favouring the zame.
The which I have alwiz allowed, and many's
the time I've zed ez much. 'Jane Vaggis,'
I've zed, 'may have acted a bit contrary in
hur life, zich ez tha wearing o' roses at mis-
taken moments, but taken ez a corpse, hur
did hur dooty, hur looked hur part.' Not thet
I would ever act contrary tu them ez Natur
hed less vavoured at zich times ; and when
my pore moather came tu the last, and what
wi' dropsy and wan thing and tother, hur wez
moast tha size o' tha feather-bed that hur
layed on, 'Moather,' I zed, 'if yer 'ave a
fancy in coffins, zay the wud and I woant
go for tu deny 'ee.' 'Martha,' hur answered,
'ony colour but black, and let the handles
ba shiny ; ' and I guved hur hallum [1] picked
out wi' brass, and ther ain't a corpse in tha
parish ez wez burried more comfortabul. But
ther," she added as she rose from her seat, "I
must be gettin' along 'ome ; law bless us ! "
she exclaimed, looking down on Joe, " how
turribul bad the pore chil does look ; but

[1] Elm.

there, ha iz gwaying tu a home o' light, tho'
I alwiz reckoned mezulf thet 'eaven must ba
trying tu tha eyes. Wull, I wish 'ee good
day, Zam Tapp," she added, "and doan't
forget a tayspoonful o' the brownest o'
sugars togither wi' a tayspoonful o' tha
strongest o' brandies, and let the zame ba
tooked zitting."

"Grandfer," said the boy when the door
closed on Martha Snykes's fat, comfortable
form, "carry me tu and fraw a bit and tull
me zommat; tull me what the wordel ba like
out ther,—ba it mortal wide?"

"Ay, ay, lad," Zam answered, raising the
dying child in his arms, "wide and lonezome,
wide and lonezome."

"But windervull full o' ditches," Joe said;
"do 'ee jump they ditches, grandfer, when
yer gaws tu and fraw tu wark?"

"Naw, lad, I ba getting owld," Zam answered; "I moastly walks 'longzide."

There was silence for a moment, and then
Joe spoke. "Grandfer," he said, "do 'ee
reckon thet they knaws more about 'eaven
auver tu Merikey than they does yhere?"

"'Tiz tha tother zide o' tha wordel," the

old man answered; "maybe they zees clearer ther."

"I ba mortal wangery,[1] grandfer," Travelling Joe answered, sighing; "I reckon I cud zlape."

Zam laid the dying boy back in the old truckle-bed. "Shall I tull 'ee zommat from the Buk, lad?" he asked.

The child shivered. "Naw, grandfer," he answered, "I wid liefer bide quiet." He sank into a broken slumber, suddenly to awake with a start.

"'Tiz turribul dimmet," he exclaimed; "but," and his face brightened, "I zees things like ditches:" so saying, he died.

[1] Tired.

RAB VINCH'S WIFE

18

THE chill October dusk swept down upon the village, as it lay sheltered against a red-breasted Devonshire hill, at the foot of which, where the river meandered brown-faced and silent out among the meadows, stood Rab Vinch's cottage. The firelight crept across the threshold, throwing shadows by the way on the white-washed walls of the small kitchen, and outlining Rab's harsh passionate features as he sat and stared down on the flames. A certain peaceful quiet which reigned in the room—for Rab's wife, who was preparing the evening meal, moved softly—was broken by the sound of footsteps, and with a brief knock a man entered.

"They've brought it in murder agin lame Tom," he cried, excitedly.

Rab shifted back his chair, and his face grew grey beneath his tanned skin.

"An' tha Squoire ain't done nought!" he exclaimed.

"Eh? tha Squoire," repeated the man, turning towards him; but a sudden movement on the part of the woman prevented him from seeing Rab. "It 'pears," he continued, "thet inter tha 'sizes tha Squoire bain't no more than ony tother man; tho' ha did git a speshil doctor down from Lonnon, costing pounds an' pounds, jest tu show thet lame Tom wezn't fixed tu his chump¹ tha zame ez moast folk; but tha jidge wez vor hanging, jidges baing paid vor zich, zo hanging it's ta ba; ony down in tha vullage uz reckons ther wez more than wan pusson mixed up in that ther murder."

"Down in tha vullage they ba mazing clivvar, no doubt," the woman answered, scornfully; "but tha law ain't no vule to ba a-hanging o' hinnocent folk."

The man moved a step nearer, and laid his hand upon her arm.

"Thet ba jest wher 'ee ba wrong, Zusan Vinch," he said. "I zeed thickey corpse a vull dree hours a-vour tha perlice iver clapped eyes on it, an' twez riglar ringed round wi' fut-

¹ *Off the chump* = not quite in his right mind.

marks thet wez niver made by ony boot o' lame Tom's; eh, an' if it had not rained thet powerful spirited, tha perlice wid o' zeen 'em themzulves, blind ez tha ba. An' my wife hur zed ta me a skaur o' times, 'Tummas Wulkie,' hur's zed, why doant 'ee gaw inter Extur an' tull tha law what yer 'ave zeen wi' yer own eyes?' An' I've up an' zed tu hur, 'Naw,' zes I, ' tha law ba a catchy thing, an' like tother folk's turnips, best not meddled with.'"

An expression of fear passed over the woman's face. "Tha law ain't for the hanging o' hinnocent folk," she repeated, doggedly.

"Tha law an' tha perlice ba moast wan," the man answered with contempt, "alwiz snuffing round arter tha wrong scent, like varmer Plant's tarrier dawg. Why did Josh Tuckitt sail for Meriky tha day arter the murder? wat call had ha to ba zo mazing smart all-ta-wance? answer me that, Zusan Vinch."

"Josh Tuckitt had nought watever to do wi' it," Rab interposed, impetuously.

"How do yer coome to knaw thic?" the man asked, with a look of suspicion.

"Cuz uz wez togither that night."

There was a moment's silence, and then Susan Finch spoke.

"Why can't yer let things bide as they ba, Tummas Wulkie?" she exclaimed, passionately. "Wan wid think yer had killed tha poor man yersulf, tha way yer ba alwiz pauking tha blame on tother folk."

"'Tiz a quare thing," the man answered, turning on his heel, "that a long tongue an' a short understandin' moast times run in couples; but ther wuman wez a kind o' extry thought o' tha Almighty's, an' uz all knaw thet tiz tha way o' zich things to cost a deal more than they ba worth. An' ez for tha pauking o' tha blame on tother folk," he continued, as he opened the door and stepped out into the night, "I wid never 'ave belaved thet a dumman not more than a skaur o' months merried wid o' bin zo zet on tha hanging o' a pore natrel; but ther women ba contrary critters, turrible zet on tha squashing o' vlies, but aiting ther roast pork with tha rest."

The echo of the man's retreating footsteps

died away, and the kettle seemed to hiss more loudly in the silence that fell upon the little kitchen. At last Rab spoke.

"Hanging ba a stuffy death," he said, hoarsely—"a mortal stuffy death."

She knelt down beside him. "Twez an accident," she whispered; "yer ba thet strong 'ee doant alwiz knaw."

"Yer ba a riglar dumman wi' yer haccidents, haccidents," he interrupted, with fierce contempt; "ain't I towld 'ee a skaur o' times thet 'twezn't no haccident."

"An' lame Tom?" she asked, falteringly.

"Lame Tom wezn't in it."

"Nor Josh Tuckitt?"

"Naw, nor Josh Tuckitt."

"O God, Rab!" she exclaimed. He drew away from her, but she, bending forward, let her face droop upon his knee. The tall clock in the corner ticked on towards night, and the kettle boiled over, but the man and the woman heeded neither: he was dimly conscious that her hot tears were falling upon his hand, but when she spoke her voice seemed far away.

"Rab," she said, "an' zoon ther wull ba dree o' uz."

He turned and looked at her, and his face softened, and an expression of pity came into his fierce, deep-set eyes.

"Little Moather," he said.

She clung to him with passionate vehemence. "'There cud niver ba no tother man but yer for me, Rab," she sobbed—"niver, niver, whatever 'ee did."

His muscular hands closed round her with a rare tenderness, and great beads of sweat gathered upon his forehead.

"What made 'ee gaw for to do it when uz wez that happy?" she said.

His lips trembled, as if he were about to speak, but he did not answer her.

"Rab," she cried, with a sudden shiver, "things dursn't bide ez they ba; they dursn't, they dursn't."

His whole expression changed, the fierce look returned to his eyes.

"Dursn't?" he repeated, in a voice of rising anger; "who axed 'ee for yer 'pinion wan way or tother?"

She did not answer him, and a silence fell

between them, till with a sudden rush of
suspicion the thought came to Rab that she
was condemning him.

"What ba 'ee a-thinking of?" he asked,
fiercely.

"Rab," she said, in her soft, low voice, as
she rubbed the lapel of his brown velveteen
coat with her hand, "I wez ony reckoning
thet twezn't for nought thet our Lord coomed
inter tha wordel feeble in body; twezn't for
nought thet Ha let Simon o' Cyrene carry
tha cross up tha steep hill to Golgotha; it
bain't tha strong who's tu lane on tha wake."
She stopped a moment, and he looked down
on her upturned face with a curious mixture
of pity, tenderness, and irritation.

"'Ee ba powerful anxious to git me ter
'Eaven, wan way or tother," he said, with a
grim smile.

"Rab," she answered, taking his great
knotted hands and pressing them against her
breast, "I widn't 'ave 'ee act contrary to
tha best thet ba in 'ee, tez ony thic, tiz ony
thic; and O Rab, if yer had zeen lame Tom
ez I did when tha perlice tooked him, his
vace thet scart wi' fear, ha might 'a been

a poor dumb critter caught in wan o' yer snares."

"Lame Tom ba wakezome," he said, and his voice trembled.

"Yes," she repeated—"wakezome, mortal wakezome."

He looked past her at the closed door, as if his sight could pierce the wooden panels and see the world that lay beyond, and into his rugged passionate face there came a certain expression of nobleness. "Mayba I wull," he began; but she, following a train of thoughts of her own, interrupted him.

"Twid ba the zame ez if yer wez to let a chile die for 'ee," she said, in a slow, dreamy voice, speaking as one who had seen a vision.

He thrust her from him and rose to his feet: "Then I wull gi' mezulf up ta-marrer," he said; "but ez for 'ee," he added, with concentrated bitterness, "yer ba no wife o' mine from this hour," and he turned from her and climbed the rickety stairs that led to their bedroom. But he could not sleep, and the slow hours passed away, and then he heard the door open softly, and by-and-by her little cold form crept into the bed and lay down beside him, and she, thinking that he slept, rested her head up against his shoulder and sobbed comfortlessly. He remained stiff and silent, as if the deafness of sleep was upon him; but his memory had travelled back to a day in their mutual childhood, the day on which he had first seen her cry. She had told her fortune on the long quaking-grasses, and had wept because Fate had ordained that she should marry a tinker; and though he had been but six years old at the time, and his mind little troubled with the thought of maidens, yet, because her weeping had been very heavy, he had promised to marry her himself, and she had been comforted. And now as he lay angry and resentful beside her, the old distich rang in his brain—tinker, tailor, soldier, sailor, rich-man, poor-man, apothecary, thief; tinker, tailor. Then a sudden rush of tenderness came to him, and he put out his hand and touched her; but she had fallen asleep.

With the first streak of dawn he rose and drew back the lattice, so that the light fell upon her face with its curves that tilted up-

wards, as the petals of some flower that seeks
its happiness in the sun, and he noticed over
again that her chestnut hair had a glint on
it like the breast of a cock pheasant.   Her
nightdress had fallen open at the neck, making visible the curves of her bosom, rounded
with coming motherhood, and he remembered with an exceeding bitterness that he
must also part from his child; but as he
looked at the woman lying there, his face
softened.

" Mayba I widn't gaw for tu do lame Tom
no harm," he said, " if her wezn't thet turribel
meddlezome; tain't dying I ba a-feard of—
I reckon I can die tha zame ez ony tother
man; but I doant want tu ba vustled[1] inter
it; but hurs a riglar wumman all-over, pushing 'ee t'wards 'Eaven wi' hur 'eart an' pulling 'ee back wi' hur tongue.   But ther, tain't
no good talking; mayba hur'll larn when 'tis
too late."

He turned away and crept softly down the
old, creaky stairs: below, in one corner of
the kitchen, there stood a big box in which
lived his two ferrets, Cross-eyes and Poley:

[1] Fussed.

he gave them their usual breakfast of bread
and milk, and let them play for a moment
about his neck. Then he took down his guns,
one by one, from the great beam against
which they rested: there was the old muzzle-
loader on which he had first learnt to shoot,
"a riglar terror to kick, but mortal depend-
zome for a right and left"; and the long
duck-gun that had carried straight in its time
—it was a family heirloom, and his great
grandfather had carried it on the night he
had been pixie-led; and, lastly, there was
Rab's own favourite gun, a pin-fire breech-
loader that had once belonged to the young
Squire. Rab took each gun in turn and
rubbed the barrel tenderly with an old oil
rag, and then returned it to its former resting-place; his big yellow lurcher stood
watching him with eyes that in their
alertness curiously resembled Rab's own.
When he had finished he tied up the dog,
and, going out, shut the door of his cottage
behind him.

A rough sob rose in his throat. "I didn't
reckon her wid zlape like thic," he said; "but
ther, women be alwiz contrary."

Up through the great woods he went, for
his road to the town lay that way. And in
a certain hedge facing west a hare had made
its seat. Rab had often tried to catch it, but
the hare had been too wary for him, and now
as he passed the accustomed spot he stopped
instinctively, and noticed that the snare had
been brushed away but that the animal had
escaped. He knelt down and reset the wire,
and as he did so he heard footsteps, and looking up he saw his wife. The blood rushed
into his face, but he assumed an air of indifference. "I reckon I've alwiz zet thickey
snare a deal too low," he said, bending down
over his work; "a hare howlds hiz 'ead wondervul 'igh when ha ba movetting along
unconscious. Eh," he continued, drawing
a deep breath, "but hares ba vantysheeny [1]
baistesses; skaurs o' times I've ruckeed [2]
down behind a bit o' vuzz wi' tha moon
a-glinting a-tap o' me and cock-leert [3] jest
on tha creep an' iverything thet quiet
'ee cud moast a-yhear tha dew a-valling;
eh, an' I've 'ad tha gun a-zide o' me an'

---

[1] Showy, handsome.   [2] Stooped down low.
[3] Dawn.

cudn't vire cuz they baistesses wez thic van·
tysheeny."

But she only saw that an animal caught in
such a snare would be hung.

"Come away, Rab," she cried; "come
away."

He looked down at the snare meditatively.

"Zome o' 'em," he said, half to himself,
"makes a to-do, but moast die mortal quiet."

"O Rab! come away," she repeated in a
voice of agony; "come away."

"Ba 'ee afraid I shull ba late for tha hang·
ing?" he cried, and sprang to his feet; then
without waiting for her answer he rushed
past her and was hidden from view behind
the thick trees.

"Rab!" she called, running after him,
"Rab! Rab! Rab!"

But there came no reply: later in the day
she learned that he had surrendered himself
to the police, but permission to see him was
refused. So when evening came she crept
homewards alone through the great woods,
and when she had reached the spot where he
had set the snare, she heard a strange cry:
the hare had been caught in the wire. Cov-

ering her ears with her hands she fled away, yet ever and ever the cry followed her.

. . . . . .

It was the day of Rab's trial: the court was crowded, and the counsel for the defence in despair; to all questions as to his motive for the crime Rab had maintained a dogged silence.

"Twezn't no haccident," he repeated; "I did it o' puppuss."

He cut short the trial by pleading guilty, and the judge, following the usual formula, rose, and having taken the black cap, turned to the prisoner and asked if he had anything to say why the sentence of death should not be passed upon him.

The ensuing silence was broken by the sound of a woman's voice. "Yer honour," Susan Finch said, for it was she who spoke, " they tull me that tha law ba agin a woman testifying for hur husband; but ther ba thic thet ba higher than the law, an' thet ba Nater; and it ain't in nater thet a woman shid zee the man thet hur loves, an' who hur knaws tu ba hinnocent—tain't in nater, I zay, thet hur shid zee him given auver

to death an' hur not to up and zay tha truth.
An' I tull yer honour the zame ez I wid tull
tha Almighty if I stud a-vor' His throne, thet
twezn't no murder Rab did thickey night;
twez an haccident, an' don't ee iver gaw for
to believe nought else. Yer doant knaw Rab
tha zame ez I do; uz wez chiles togither, an'
they thet ba chiles togither kind o' larns
wun-an-tother's hearts unconscious. Rab
bain't tha sort thet takes to murder, Rab
ain't; ha's tempestuous o' times, an' thic
strong thet ha doesn't alwiz knaw, but his
heart is ez tenderzome ez a chil's. I cud tull
'ee a skaur o' things, on'y Rab aint wan o'
they ez likes to ba boasted of; but I ax yer
honour why ba Rab a-standing a-vor' ee at
this yhere blessid minit? Did the perlice
catch him?—naw; then why ba ha a-stand·
ing ther a-vor' ee, wi' they cruel iron things
on the hands o' 'em? Why, becuz Lame
Tom ba wakezome: ther bain't no tother
lad thet wid up an put tha rope round hiz
neck rather then anything wakezome shid
suffer unjust. But ther baint no call for a
rope, and if Rab wid ony spake ha cud tull
'ee zo hiszulf. An' if yer ax me why ha

19

hezn't stud up vrom tha vust an' zed it twez
an haccident, then I tull 'ee it was becase I
wez alwiz a-worritting o' him thet kept him
to zilence. I wez alwiz a-axing questions,
an' ha doan't like it, an' ha wants tu larn
me. I've done a power o' thinkin' zince
thickey marning Rab gi'ed hiszulf up, an'
I've reckoned it all out. I wez too mortal
anxious tu show him tha way, an' Rab ain't
no wumman tu ba showed things. Ha likes
tu do hiz right hiz own way—ha doan't want
no wan tu larn him; an' I wez alwiz a-zay-
ing, yer dursn't do thic an' yer must do thet,
zo ha ba jest a-larning o' me; but, O Rab!"
she ended, in a voice of passionate entreaty,
turning to him, "I've larned, I've larned;
ony tull 'em—*tull* 'em."

When the woman ceased speaking a silence
fell upon the court, and the eyes of all there
turned to the prisoner. Rab's harsh obstinate
face had grown grey beneath the tanned skin;
his lips, pressed one on the other with the
grip of a vice, looked as if no power could
ever force them to unclose: then his eyes
met those of his wife, and with a convulsive
effort he spoke. " 'Twez done temperzome,"

he exclaimed, brokenly—"powerful temper-zome; ha said thic thet wez baisteous o' hur," and Rab pointed with his hand in the direction of his wife. "Mayba," he con-tinued, huskily, "if yer cud find Josh Tuck-itt, ha cud make things look a bit better for me."

WIDDER VLINT

WIDDER VLINT'S cottage stud at the tap o' the vullage, wi' a banging girt vlight o' staps a-vor the door. The staps wez brauken an' mortal zlippery when it rained; but thet wezn't here nor there, cuz vew folks iver came up 'em. Widder Vlint, hur wez disrespactit in the vullage, 'aving borned dree drunkards, tho' the naybours wez kind o' zorry vor hur now an' agin; an' when hur zon Josh wez drawed vrom hiz hoss an' brauk hiz neck, they jest zed that " wan o' the tu wez drunk," an' left folk to judge atween the man an' the mare.

Wan arternoon I drapped in to zee how hur wez getting on, cuz ther wez a moast kindiddlin'[1] zmell o' fried bacon cooming droo the door. The table wez layed for tay, zo I zat mezulf down. I wez a kind o' relation o' Widder Vlint's, tho' I didn't make much o'

[1] Enticing.

it 'zept at mait times an' zich, cuz o' hur baing
so mortal disrespactit.   It zeemed to me hur
didn't take anuff count o' the 'pinion o' the
vullage, hur wez thic turrible zet on her childer, women not 'aving no discarnment in zich
things.   Wull, I 'adn't bin vive minets inzide
the door vor hur got talkin' o' 'em, tho' I
didn't vind no speshul intrast in the subject
mezulf.

"I've a deal to be thankvul vor, a deal,"
hur zed.   "Ther wez Tummas, now,"—then
hur stapped quat[1]; I reckon 'twez 'ard even
vor hur to vind anything vavourzome to zay
o' Tummas.   "Wull," hur dawdled on, "ha
had a windervul 'ead o' hair, had Tummas.
Pore lad ! ha wez alwez a good lad to me;
ha braut me the vurst shillun that iver ha
arned, an' thin ha kinder tuk it back.   Ha
aimed high, did Tummas, tho' maybe ha
didn't alwez raitch."

Hur wez zilent a minet an' tarned the bacon
in the pan where twez spittin' an' zmellin'
moast amazin' tasty.

"Then there wez Josh," hur contineed, "ha
thet wez drawed vrom hiz hoss an' brauk hiz

[1] Plump.

neck. IIa had a wondervul kindiddlin zmile o'
times had Josh, an' when they braut him 'ome
to me the last time an' layed him down in the
corner o' the kitchen, thickey zmile wez on
his vace kind o' pacevul like. I stapped a-zide
him droo the night; I thought maybe the
pore chil' might find it lonesome out ther wi'
iverything so noo. I tooked his hand cuz
twez dark vust a-long, an' Josh wez alwez
mortal a-feardt o' the dark. An' I kind o'
thought ez how ha wez ez a little lad, I
knawed ha hadn't alwez acted zactly vor the
best zince he had grawed to be a man. The
moon riz an' staled in upon him an' ha zmiled
back at hur, an' twez a turrible pacevul zmile
thic ha guved hur. An' thin ther coomed to
me they words vrom the Buk, 'Gaw in pace,
vor thy zins be vorguved to 'ee.' An' I vell
a-sobbing, quiet-like, cuz I didn't want to dis-
tarb him, pore lamb, but ha jest zmiled on.
The pace o' the Laurd ain't like our pace, it
ain't to be brauk, it ain't to be brauk."

Hur stapped short an' wan banging girt
tear fell strat in the pan. I thort twez a
mortal pity to spile good bacon zo, speshul
ez Josh wez the biggest rapscalliou thet ever

walked; but I cudn't help baing a bit zorry
vor the pore owld dumman, cuz 'tis the way
wi' women to git turrible vond o' trash.

"Jesse was the next to gaw," hur zed, after
hur had kind o' come to hurself like, "my
little lad dead now along o' the rast!" Hur
alwez called Jesse "hur little lad," tho' ha wuz
vull sax veet high an' weighed nigh on vour-
teen stone; but women ain't got no discrum-
ination in zich things.

"Wull, wull," hur ended up, "I've only
Dave luft now, but ha be a vine upstanding
lad, an' I've a deal to be thankvul vor, a
deal."

Then the big clock in the corner struck sax,
an' Dave coomed in, an' I wez moast mortal
glad to see him, cuz the bacon wez jest ready
to be dished, an' I niver cud a-bear things
burnt to a cinder. "Moather," ha zed ez ha
hunged up hiz tools behind the door, "'ee
have got on thickey boots thet coom zo hard
on yer little taw."

"Wull, Dave, lad," hur answered, "I wez
a gwaying to buy a noo pair ez I pramised
'ee I wid, only I erned[1] up agin Maister

---

[1] Ran.

Parsons, ha ez kapes the little grocer's shap down the lower end o' the vullage, an' ha zed ez how ha had got a powerzome noo tay in, cuz I towld him ez how yer didn't vind anuff scratt[1] in thickey last thet uz 'ad, zo I thort I wud jest buy a pun an' let the boots bide a bit."

" Wull, moather," ha zed ez ha pulled his cheer up to the table, "I do zeem a moast windervul 'and at rizzing a tharst, but zome-how"—an' ha pushed hiz cup acrass to be vulled agin—" it zeems ez if ther wez thic in the tharst thet tay didn't git houldt of, but 'tis a powerzome gud tay, an' moast vull o' scratt all-the-zame."

I saw hur look zmart down at hiz plate— ha hadn't tiched a bit o' victuals, ony drunk away ez if his throat wez a red 'ot coal. 'Pon me Zam, I cud amoast yhear it fizz where I zat.

" Ate a bit o' bacon like a gud chil'," hur zed, kindiddlin' like; " 'tis from the ztreaky end."

"It zmells windervul tasty, moather," ha answered, "an' I wid dearly like a bit o' it

[1] Scrape.

cold ta-marrer; but the tay iz zo powerzome gud, I doan't zeem to care for naught ulse."

Later on, when the table had been cleared an' iverything made vitty,[1] uz all drawed our cheers up to the vire. Widder Vlint hur tooked hur knittin' vrom the drawer in the owld dresser, an' when I yhear'd thickey naydles clacking away, I claused my eyes an' reckoned I wud gaw to slape. After a bit Dave ha turned to the owld dumman—

"Moather," ha zed, "do 'ee dap back on thic night when pore Jesse got kind o' mad wi' tha drink an' shat hizsulf, an' how yer an' me wint out 'and in 'and an' vound him, an' yer tarned to me an' zed, 'I've ony thee luft now, Dave'; an' I tooked pore Jesse's hand an' layed it atween yers an' mine, an' zwore thet I wid niver touch strong drink, an' if I had to die vor it I wid die game? Moather, moather," he ended up kind o' sharp like, "I reckon the drink 'ull 'ave me yet."

Hur put hur arms round him an' drawed hiz head down upon hur lap, ez maybe hur had done many times a-vor when ha wez a little lad.

[1] Right.

"Pore lamb!" hur zed, "pore lamb!"

Arter a bit hur contineed, "Dave," hur zed, "do 'ee mind on the pore widdy wuman in the Buk, an' how she guved her mite to the Laurd, an' tho' ther wez urch[1] volks alongside o' hur ez guved gorgeus gufts, yit the Laurd Ha valleyed the mite moast. An' zo I reckon 'tiz wi' uz—'tain't wat uz does, but wat uz tries to do, that the Laurd vallys, an' thin Ha kind o' makes up the rast Hizsulf."

But Dave ha ony gripped howldt o' the pore dumman more tight like. "Moather, moather," ha zed, "spose I shudn't die game?"

Hur rinned hur vingers droo hiz hair kind o' tender vashion, but hur didn't zay naught. I reckon mezulf hur wez thunkin' thet 'twad be wi' ha the zame ez 'twez wi' the rast o' 'em.

"Zay zommat, moather, zay zommat," ha axed.

Hur looked away acrass hiz hed inter the vire, ez if hur zaw zomethin' mazin' particular down amung the coals.

[1] Rich.

" Dave," hur answered, kind o' zlow, " when vust I coomed to be disrespactit in the vullage, an' folks drawed it at me that I had borned dree drunkards, it zeemed a bit hard, tho' I cudn't gaw vor to lay blame on the lads. Then Tummas wez tuk, an' the naybours wez a bit sniffy an' thin. Claus on tap o' ha, pore Josh ha brauk his neck, an' tho' the folks coomed to the vuneral, they kind o' made a vavour o' it. Wull, then, Jesse ha shat hizsulf, an' I bought the hatbands an' gluves, an' they wez real gud uns too, but no wan wez ther to put 'em on, an' uz waited an' they niver coomed, zo yer an' I uz wint on a-lone. An' ez I walked a-longside o' 'ee Dave, the strait it niver seemed zo long a-vor or the vullage zo full o' folk. An' when I passed thickey hauses, I kinder zed to mezulf ain't ther wan pusson in 'ee that wull coom out an' voller me lad. Then uz tarned the corner where Mat Mucksey's hause stands, an' I thought he wud coom surely, vor they played togither ez little lads. An' ha stud at the winder an' looked out, an' I kind o' gripped howldt o' him wi' my eyes. I thort maybe the Laurd wud let me draw him so, but twezn't to be. Then me heart wez anger't that they shud sarve my boy zo, my lamb, my little lad, my Jesse, an' I didn't yhear naught o' the sarvice, tho' ther be terrible comforting words in it, but I tooked my boy an' layed him ther on the disrespactit north zide, where the zun only creeps round o' whiles; but maybe the Laurd will think on thic when the Jidgment day cooms an' riz him tenderer accordin'. An' Dave, why shud yer want to be more than ha, pore lamb, pore lamb?—wezn't ha the uldest, an' why shud yer want to make yerzulf higher?"

Dave ha looked up in hur vace, but hur kind o' tarned her eyes tother way.

"Moather," ha zed, "yer wudn't 'ave me die a drunkard, surely?"

But hur didn't answer ha at all.

"Moather, moather," ha zed.

"Dave," hur zed, "didn't I borne 'ee all, didn't 'ee all lay upon my brast, an' ain't 'ee all my childer, an' why shud wan gaw vor to make hizsulf higher than tothers?"

Dave ha drapped hiz head down on hur knay, an' the kitchen wez zilencevul.

At last ha lifted up hiz vace, an' twez

a windervul pitying luk ha gived her. " Moather," ha zed, " I reckon uz zons 'ave brought 'ee a power o' zarrar." [1]

But hur answered kind o' random like. " Dave," hur zed, " God vorgive me an' make 'ee do wat iz vitty."

.   .   .   .   .   .

When the winter coomed round, Widder Vlint hur kind o' vell togither. The naybours zed, " Hur hadn't no more spirit than a warm, an' vor sich drearysome folk warms wez the best company." Then hur tooked to hur bed, an' wan Vriday marning hur wez thet bad Dave didn't gaw to hiz work, but zat azide hur droo the day, an' I kind o' kapt him company. Hur dauzed a bit, an' when hur wauk up Dave axed hur if hur had any pain.

" No, lad," hur answered, " wangery,[2] turrible wangery, thics all."

Just about vour o' the clock hur zeemed a bit brighter.

" Dave," hur zed, " I reckon I wid like a chapter vrom the Buk."

" Shall I vetch it, moather ? " he axed.

---

[1] Sorrow.   [2] Tired.

"No, lad," she zed. "I misremembered it wez down-stairs; maybe yer cud zay a prayer?"

"I ony knaws 'Our Vather' an' the Blessin', moather," he answered.

"Then I reckon 'tiz the Blessin' I wull 'ave," she zed; "'tiz a bootivul zaying, 'Vor wat us 'ave recaved'—zay on, lad."

"The Laurd make uz truly thankvul," Dave ended.

"An' uz 'ave 'ad a deal to be thankvul vor, a deal," hur zed.

But Dave ha jest zat ther like a stone an' didn't zay naught.

"Zay, lad, zay," hur axed, kind o' painvul.

Thin ha tooked hur hands, mazing owld an' knotted hands they wez, ha tooked 'em in hiz an' ha kneeled azide the bed an' put his vace down agin hur heart.

"Moather, moather," he zed, "God guved me thee."

Hur only spoke wance after thic. "Lay me zide o' Jesse," hur zed; "I reckon the little lad 'ull be warmer along o' hiz moather."

DAVE

SPRAWLING down one hill and half-way up another was a little village; at the corner of its main street stood the White Lion Inn. The sun poured yellow light through the bar windows on to the sanded floor, and on the figures of two men who sat talking at a table.

"I tell you he's sweet on my cousin Phœbe, damn him," exclaimed the younger man, bringing his fist down on the table.

"And what's that got to say to it?" replied the other, in a slow, heavy voice. "Josh Tuckett 'ull never see no darter o' his married to a drunkard."

"Dave ain't no drunkard; he takes his glass and goes out. Dang him, I wish he wor."

The elder man leant forward and caught hold of the button of his companion's coat.

"Answer me this, Tummas Rod," he said, "didn't his father die o' drink?"

"Ay, sure."

"And his grandfather afore him?"

"Ay, certain."

"Bain't his three brothers lying in the churchyard at this very minnit reg'lar soaking the place wi' spirits; the grass niver growed casual over their graves the same as it did over t'other folks'."

"What's that got to do wi' Dave?"

"Why, begore, he'll come to the like sooner or later, mark my words if he don't. He's a drunkard now—at heart. Scores o' times I've reckoned to hear his throat split and crack when the drink dizzles down it."

A heavy flush rose to Rod's face. "And may it; the sooner the better," he said.

"You and he were thick anuff as boys," replied the old man, rising, and regarding him curiously.

Rod turned away and went back to the bar. "Didn't I tell 'ee that he be sweet on my cousin and her on him," he answered, in a sullen voice.

There was a sound of footsteps, and Dave

entered, the old man taking his departure at the same time. Rod glanced with quick scrutiny at the newcomer's gaunt but boyish face, as, dropping his bag of tools, he flung sixpence on the counter.

"A half-and-half, Tom," he said. "My throat ba reglar dring'd [1] wi' thirst."

The flush on Rod's face receded, leaving it ash-grey. He filled a small glass to the brim with spirits, and pushed it across the bar. Dave swallowed the contents at a gulp, and stood, fingering the glass nervously.

"Take another nip," said Rod.

"Naw, wan ba anuff, thank 'ee."

"Come, I'll stand yer."

Dave's thin white face reddened. "I dursn't," he said, turning away and picking up his bag of tools.

The innkeeper burst into a rough laugh. "You puts me in mind of a maid before her first kiss, terrible afraid, but wonderful willing," he replied. "Come," he urged, unsteadily, "drink me success to something I've set my mind on."

There was silence a moment. "Ba it zum-

[1] Squeezed up.

mat pertikler speshil?" Dave asked at length.

"I told 'ee I'd set my mind on it."

"Drink ba kindiddling temptsome," Dave muttered, half to himself, as he watched Rod fill two glasses with spirits. "Wull," he added, gulping down the spirits with fever- ish impatience, "may 'ee git wat 'ee want and more."

Rod looked at him a moment, his lips twitching: "To the damnation of Dave Vlint, body and soul!" he exclaimed, and draining the glass, flung it across the bar at the wall opposite. For a moment the two men regarded each other in silence; then Dave turned on his heel, halted a moment at the door, and glanced back,—"Did 'ee mean they wuds?" he said.

"Twor nort but a bit o' fun," Rod an- swered, forcing a laugh.

"Ther ain't nort speshil vantysheeny[1] in sich jokes," replied Dave, and going out he left Rod alone. He made his way through the street, and up the hill behind the village, where the pine-trees stood massing them-

Showy.

selves against the blue sky like heavy blue-
green clouds. Leaving the road, he entered
the wood by a footpath. It was autumn;
the ground was strewn with cones; overhead
the wind soughed with the sound of the sea.
Standing beside a broken stile was a girl;
her chestnut hair, escaping from the kerchief
that bound it, rippled and curled about her
neck and forehead. Dave started when he
saw her, and advanced more slowly. She
came towards him, and they stood together:
she was not tall, "about as high as his
heart."

"What's come to 'ee Dave!" she exclaimed,
in a soft, guttural voice; "it's dree weeks
since you've bin a-nigh me."

He was silent, averting his eyes as if he
were afraid to look into hers.

"You made me love 'ee, you made me love
'ee," she burst out, her voice trembling; "and
now——"

"Phœbe, lass, 'tis better that I bide
away."

"You shud 'ave thought o' that afore," she
said, bitterly.

"Ay, sartin I shud."

She caught hold of the two lapels of his coat,—"Dave, Dave," she cried, "you don't love me arter all; and you swore me true down by the Wishing Well."

"I didn't love 'ee then the zame as I do now by a deal," he answered, taking her hands in his.

"Oh lad, I can't fathom 'ee," she said, with a sob.

"Sweetheart, 'tis the drink I'm afeard of; 'twull have me wan day like did my vather and brothers afore me."

"But I bain't afeard."

"I might be cruel hard on 'ee, lass," he said, pressing her hands tight against his broad chest. "A man can't answer for his-sulf when the drink's upon him."

Her dark grey eyes filled with tears. "But I bain't afeard, Dave," she reiterated. "I bain't afeard."

He looked at her with great tenderness. "I dursn't, dear heart; I dursn't," he said, and his voice shook.

"Ther wud ba the times atween whiles," she urged.

Turning from her, he caught hold of a tree-bough and steadied himself. "Lass, lass, don't put me in mind o' 'em."

"You ain't loving me the zame as you did, or 'ee wudn't need no minding," she exclaimed, brokenly. "And I ain't fallen off in looks." She came round the tree, stood in front of him, and unbinding her kerchief, shook her thick chestnut hair about her shoulders. "See, Dave," she continued, "it's vine and long for all it loses in the curl; and my voot too, Dave,"—she kicked off her shoe,—"'tis wonderful arched, and a deal smaller than the young ladies' up to the great House. My arms, Dave,"—she slipped back her sleeve,—"they might be a chile's, they're that bedimpled."

Stopping abruptly, she burst into tears,— "Oh, lad, lad," she sobbed, "you bain't look-ing, you bain't looking."

He let go the branch of the tree, took her in his arms, and drew her close up against his breast. He put back her head with gentle force, and kissed her mouth and eyes, her throat and bosom. As they stood molten in one mould, there came down the wind the sound of children's laughter: hearing it,

the man and woman fell trembling, then
apart.

They stood staring at each other like two
people guilty of a crime.

"There ba them that might ba born arter
us," he said, hoarsely.

She watched the sudden hardening of his
mouth. "Must us mind on 'em?" she pleaded—"must us mind on 'em?"

"I cud niver fo'ce no chile o' ours to bear
wat I've bin fo'ced to bear," he answered;
"'twad ba devil's wark—I cudn't do it."

Her face grew white and hopeless. "I
can't feel for the childer, I ain't no mother
yet," she said, brokenly.

Desire shook him: he looked at her slight
form that seemed to tremble into womanhood before his eyes, then, with an abrupt
cry, he turned and left her.

She flung herself down and wept,—
through the trees her wailing followed him,
yet his heart cried out so loudly that he
knew not if the wailing came from her lips
or his own. Long he wandered in the wood,
but when night fell returned again to his
cottage. Pushing open the door, the moon-

light streaming in after him, he entered the small kitchen. On the table, the cork withdrawn, was a bottle of spirits,—the air reeled with the smell of it. He did not know whose hand had placed the bottle there, but his harsh thirst demanded slaking, and forced him forward. Clutching at his throat, striving to tear the thirst from it, he advanced—the bottle glistening in the moonlight, looking as if it were alive. He cast an agonised glance round the walls, seeking help from familiar things, and his eyes fell on his gun. A sob of relief broke from him : he took down the gun, loaded it hurriedly, the smell of the spirits dripping on to his lips, he licking it down. He snatched the bottle from the table, shouldered his gun, and went out,—up through the woods, past the broken stile, where the coarse grass lay pressed close to the earth and Phœbe had flung herself down and wept. With averted face he passed the spot, and entered deep into the heart of the wood. At last he stopped : about him the trees grew close and thick, no eye but God's could see his shame. He leant his gun up against a branch; the moonlight edged itself between the trees, and he held the bottle up to it.

"So yer have got the best o' me at last," he said,—"yer have got the best o' me at last."

The bottle glistened : he brought it nearer his lips, his thirst pressed for quenching, the thirst that he would slake before he shot himself.

"Yer smiling devil," he burst out, with sudden fierceness, "yer reckon to catch me, do 'ee. No, by hell! yer don't; I'll die wi'out tasting 'ee," and he dashed the bottle into fragments at his feet. A moment later he had flung himself upon the ground, striving to lick up the spirits with his tongue.

"Dog that I ba, dog that I ba," he sobbed. "No better than a dog—no better than a dog."

Sick with shame and horror, he regained his feet: he took a piece of cord from his pocket, made a loop in it, attaching one end to the trigger of the gun. He pressed the cold steel barrel up against his hot beating heart, and placed his foot in the loop. "A dog's death for a dog," he muttered.

The moonlight shone on him, on the gun, and on the broken bottle at his feet: the glistening glass attracted him and he stared at it, fresh thoughts crowding his brain. A tremor ran through him : raising his eyes, he fixed them on the moonlit heavens and grey wind-spun clouds. "Ther ba zommat in me a'zide the dog," he said, slowly. "Ay, be-gore, I'll live game, I'll zee it droo," and drawing himself together, he turned his face once more on life.

www.ingramcontent.com/pod-product-compliance
Lightning Source LLC
Chambersburg PA
CBHW020808060726
47498CB00017B/962